WAR MAGE

EXTENDED EDITION

L. A. JACOB

Cover artwork © by Marc Ducrow
marcducrowart.com

Cover design copyright © by Niki Lenhart
nikilen-designs.com

Published by Water Dragon Publishing
waterdragonpublishing.com

ISBN 978-1-957146-23-2 (Trade Paperback)

10 9 8 7 6 5 4 3 2 1

FIRST EDITION

This work of fiction takes place in Afghanistan in 2004. Some of the places existed at the time and some never existed. This novel is based on the available research I could find on the Internet and from memoirs of soldiers who have been there at different times.

Again, as with *Homecoming*, if there is anything glaringly wrong or spot on, please contact me through my website: *lajacob.com*. You can also sign up for my mailing list to be notified of other stories and novels.

Enjoy.

WAR MAGE

AFGHANISTAN, 2004

1

THE AFGHAN NATIONAL POLICE seemed to like wasting American ammo. First Magus Brent Rogers assumed that was why the ANP were shooting up a vineyard half a kilometer away.

"Whoa, whoa, whoa!" yelled Sergeant Custer, storming up the observation hill. The rest of the team scampered up behind him. "Wizard!"

Brent got to the top of the hill just after Custer and handed him a black stone with gold Pashtun symbols on it. Whoever held the stone could speak and understand the language on the stone.

Custer yelled, "What the fuck you doing?" Any trigger-happy Afghan could hear him, Brent thought. But the Afghans were having too much fun mowing down vines from a distance.

The Afghans and Custer's men all stood at the top of a small, fortified hill. Piled about three feet high, directly in front of them, lay sandbags, the ANP standing over the makeshift wall, firing across a dirt path into the vineyard. Most of the vines were already cut down, exposing a small dirty-red hut with glassless holes for windows just beyond.

Some Afghans paused to reload. Custer grabbed one man by the shoulder, yanking him away from the wall and his semi-automatic weapon. Seeing this, the one next to him paused and stepped away from his SAW. So did the one next to him, soon ending the fire down the short line of ten Afghans. A potshot rang out, and someone out in the vineyard yelled. Custer glared at the men, who looked sheepish.

"What the fuck is going on?"

One of the Afghans spoke, but Brent didn't understand him. The man gestured to the vineyard. Brent thought he caught the word "Taliban."

"Where is he?" Custer demanded, as he rose to peer out at the vineyard.

No one shot back at them, though they were big enough targets, standing over the wall of sandbags. Brent began the "Raise the Enemy" spell. A boy, flailing, rose from behind the hut. They heard him screaming.

Custer yelled, "Don't shoot —", but someone on the line took a clear shot at him.

The boy stopped moving and fell with a thud to the ground.

"Who did that — find out who did that!" A hard-eyed Afghan said something, but Custer wasn't buying it. "We could have talked to him."

The Afghan snorted and said something else. Custer went red.

"Sarge's gonna pop," said Mark, backing away.

"Shut up," whispered Jason, watching the sergeant, ready to step in if necessary. They couldn't see Custer's eyes behind his sunglasses, but Brent saw the fury by his body language alone.

Sergeant Robert James Custer did pop. "You might think it's easier just to kill whoever you think is Taliban, but we're not in this fight to make things easy. That was somebody's son, and, even if he was Taliban, you just killed someone's goddamn kid. What if it was your fucking kid?"

Some of the other Afghans looked down. But the one who spoke, obvious to Brent he was a *mujahideen* — a resistance fighter during the Soviet invasion — didn't look sorry at all. In fact, he walked around the fortifications of the hill to the vineyard, his gun at the ready, all by himself.

"Dumb fuck," spat Custer, and turned to the remaining ANP. "Find out who owns that hut, now that you've mowed down his vines."

Custer handed the stone back to Brent, who dropped it into a pouch hanging off his belt. Brent looked at the Afghans, some with pockmarks and scars on their faces. Most looked young, unblemished, new to fighting against any enemy. Brent studied the ones with scars, looking for the man who tied him up and tortured him just a few short months ago.

He sometimes couldn't tell the difference between one Afghan and another. All scarred men reminded him of that time in the freezer. He rubbed his shoulder, which he allowed to ache, even though he knew a spell to take the pain away.

Brent, surprised that he got back with his old team, thought that since he blabbed all about the magic training, they would consider him a collaborator. He assumed that, at best, he would be stripped of everything and dishonorably discharged; at worst, become a permanent resident of Leavenworth prison. The Magic Corps did not press charges. He had to talk to the Army shrink, and he received new orders when she said he was fit for duty. It was like nothing had ever happened.

Custer scowled at the sun. "Let's see about the western village. We can check if the medic came by."

Jason nodded. He was Brent's backup "doc", so was often concerned about medicine. None of the Afghans wanted Brent's "sorcery." It was literally against their religion.

The western village was too small to have a name. It consisted of maybe three families, probably all connected by blood. A man sat under an overhang at one of the houses smoking a hand-rolled cigarette. Gnarled and short, he looked like the stubborn leafless trees in the front yard. He squinted at the approach of the men, but Brent saw some scurrying behind the house, black shapes moving among the orchards.

"A fine day," said Custer, holding out his hands, palms up, in the universal "We come in peace" gesture, the translation stone tucked between his thumb and forefinger. "I am Staff Sergeant Custer of the US Army."

The man's eyes moved up and down, taking him in. He puffed a bit before saying, "Timin."

Assuming that was his name, Custer continued. "I am honored to meet you. Would you mind if we take a look around?"

The man snapped something at Custer. Brent and the team knew this wasn't going to go well. A group of women came out from the back of the house, dressed in head-to-toe black *burqas*, but they did not have their eyes veiled.

Meanwhile, the old man continued to rant.

Brent did not look at the women, but Cory stared. Mark hit him, and Cory dropped his eyes momentarily. A woman stopped, but got dragged away by her companions. Cory watched her go.

"She's the ugliest bitch in the world, Cory," said Mark.

"Her eyes —"

"She ain't worth it, kid."

Brent thrust his staff lightly into the ground, trying to sense other movement. He felt the receding women, but there were more people around. A heavy foot, close by. Watching them. He turned, as if trying to see into the trees.

"Can we meet them?" Custer replied to something the man said. Brent just knew that these had to be Taliban, secret fighters, probably the ones they were looking for.

The man folded his arms across his chest and muttered. Custer forced a smile.

Brent raised his head, feeling movement through his staff. Coming over the rise behind them, he thought he could see shapes moving against the sun. Even though Brent wore sunglasses like they all did, the brutal sun forced him to shield his eyes to see. He could pick out a few men heading their way.

The interlopers were a squad of eight soldiers laden down with packs, all in tan, as opposed to the camouflage of tan and green worn by the members of Brent's team. They wore the patch of Army Special Forces — the brown arrowhead with a sword and three lightning bolts. Brent knew who they were without their signature hats: A team of Green Berets.

With them came an interpreter dressed in a hodgepodge of Afghan clothing and some military belts. He carried a military-issue pistol and holster, which Brent caught his team staring at. Brent's team didn't have sidearms like that. A scarf covered the interpreter's nose and mouth; black sunglasses hid his eyes. All of the Berets wore better sunglasses than Brent's squad.

"Sergeant," greeted one of the Green Berets. According to his stripes, he was a staff sergeant like Custer; though when he said the title, it sounded like he was in charge. Custer didn't back down.

"Sergeant," he replied.

The Beret looked at Timin. "These men bothering you?"

Through the interpreter, he said, "Yes. They come here staring at my women, and now they want my sons."

The sergeant turned to look at Custer's men. Brent did not look down from the withering glare of the Green Beret.

"Why don't you go back to base," said the sergeant to Custer. "We'll take care of things here."

"Sure," said Custer. "Are you giving us a direct order?"

Let the contest begin, thought Brent, watching the two men.

"I believe I am, Sergeant," said the Beret, leaning close. "We've been working on getting this fucker to tell us where his stash is. Don't fuck it up for us."

"Right," Custer said, and turned to his own team. "Come on."

The men turned to head back to their vehicle, a Bradley troop transport truck.

"Prick," said Mark.

"Probably pissing on their territory," said Brent. "You know how they get, especially if you do something better."

Brent felt eyes on his back and turned around. Three of the Berets watched him. One gave a pansy wave. Brent felt a fire in his chest. He almost stomped the staff down, to send an earth wave their way.

"Wizard," Custer said. "Come on."

Brent must've looked angry for Custer to round on him like that. He forced himself to look away as they went to the Bradley.

"What now?" asked Mark, settling into the driver's seat.

"We go east. There's something the old man was babbling about."

"What, Sarge?"

Custer reached over to give the translation stone to Brent. "Something your rock translated as a 'flying salamander'."

Mark laughed his big, booming laugh. "What's that guy smoking?"

"Don't know, but it won't hurt to go find out."

Brent didn't have time to think as Mark drove at near breakneck speed, confident in Brent's ability to sense IED's. Buried in the road or tripped by wires, the insurgency planted the improvised explosive devices to disrupt travel by blowing up vehicles.

Brent wondered if Mark did it on purpose to see if he could out-distance Brent's ability. After his debriefing, Brent practiced on improving his distance and speed at finding IED's. He could now sense about 100 meters in all directions; twice that if it he concentrated.

There were no IED's in the way of their trip. They turned onto a dirt road. According to the map, it was the entrance to a village named Baktar.

About five minutes in, he saw black, ruined buildings in the distance. The ground surrounding them was black and smooth instead of brown and sandy. Black nubs in the ground took the place of neat rows of crops.

As they got closer, the rock and mud houses that remained stood blackened and charred. Mark slowly drove into the village center, or what would have been, except the well was burned black.

"The fuck?" Mark whispered.

"Stop," said Custer.

He got out before the Bradley came to a full stop. Jason and Brent climbed out from the rear. Cory didn't come out initially, looking through the slits of the Bradley at the apocalyptic destruction.

It stank of fire and sulfur, the way hell would probably smell. Brent turned around in a circle for a minute, trying to use his magic to sense things of the past. He had to touch something to do it, though. He walked in the fine dirt to a blackened mud wall, touched it with his bare fingers.

It was smooth, he noticed, and closed his eyes, thinking the spell. Behind his eyes, he saw fire, like a flame thrower, come right at him. He let go, and fell backwards, stumbling.

Jason caught him. "What happened?"

"Fire," said Brent. "Directed fire."

"Sarge!" yelled Mark.

The three men ran to Mark. He stood looking at the ground. At first, Brent saw nothing but sand. But then, he saw some glittering rocks in the dirt.

Custer dug his hand in the dirt and lifted his hand, letting the fine sand flow between his fingers. He brushed some sand away and some of the rocks remained in his hand. Except they weren't rocks.

"Glass bits," said Custer, in awe.

"Seventeen-hundred degrees Fahrenheit," said Jason. He shrugged when the men stared at him. "Trivial Pursuit."

"Even flame throwers don't get that hot," said Mark

"No wonder everything's ash," said Custer. "And no wonder the old man was so scared."

"Flying salamander," mused Jason.

It came to Brent in a rush, and when it did, so did the memory of the question his torturers began with.

Brent dashed from the group and ran to the rickety side of a building. He threw up his lunch, breakfast, and maybe yesterday's dinner. He was dry-heaving when Custer patted his back and pulled out a water bottle from Brent's pack, handing it to him.

Brent couldn't trust himself to drink it. He poured some into his mouth, sloshed it around, spit it out.

He looked up at Custer and uttered one hoarse word: "Dragons."

Back at Forward Operating Base Lonestar, Cory sat in the pitch blackness along with Mark and Brent.

"Her eyes were blue," Cory was saying.

"Get her outta your head, man," admonished Brent.

"I can't. I know she was beautiful underneath."

"Islamic porn. Wrists and ankles."

Mark chuckled at the old joke.

"Fuck you," Cory snapped.

Brent heard Cory get up to fumble his way through the darkness to his cot. The main door to the Gansett container opened, spilling light onto the dirt, then disappeared when the door slammed shut.

They heard someone coming. Brent sat up straighter, the lightning spell at hand, ready to fire.

"Custer," said a voice.

Brent relaxed.

"What did the brass say?" Brent asked.

"The Green Berets got to them first," said Custer in the dark. "Brass wants to see us."

"Us?" Brent sat up. "Now?"

"At the asscrack of dawn," said Custer.

That didn't sound good. Brent got up immediately and went to his cot. He pulled out his kit to make sure he had a relatively clean uniform.

The next morning at 0510, ten minutes after the normal patrols left, they waited inside the Combat Task Force headquarters. They saluted and remained in formal stance while the major in charge of the CTF came into the office.

"You're all in a fuckload of trouble."

"Sir?" asked Custer. Still no eye contact.

"You know about our secret weapon. You —" he looked pointedly at Brent — "had to fuckin' blab about the dragons."

Brent swallowed. "It was a guess, sir."

"A guess, my ass." The major looked at Custer. "I don't want you to say one fucking word about dragons. You never saw what they did, you got it?"

"Yes, sir," said Custer with no emotion on his face.

The major looked at the other men in turn. Cory was the only one who looked away.

"Not. One. Word," repeated the major. "Dismissed."

The team left the office and Mark let out a breath. "That wasn't so bad."

Custer said, "Let's go back to that village. See if we can find any hidden stashes."

Mark grinned.

They dismounted in the village among the blackened buildings. Brent had no idea where to start. Looking at the destruction around him brought back fear. *What if the dragons came back?*

Mark and Jason examined the buildings.

Custer watched Brent. "You gonna be okay, Sergeant?"

"I don't know."

Brent stayed by the vehicle. He looked out to the south and could see a dot flying in their direction. He couldn't tell at this distance if it had wings or not.

"Wizard?" called Jason.

Brent broke from his gaze into the distance and followed the voice to the well nearby. The men gathered there, looking south, behind Brent. Brent turned around.

Where he had been looking before, a plume of black smoke now rose from the horizon. Brent looked back at the men, and then finally at Custer.

"We should go investigate," Custer said.

Mark was first back to the Bradley. As soon as they piled in, Mark floored the petal.

"Jesus, man," snapped Jason, as he got squished between Cory and Brent when the vehicle squealed onto the hard-packed dirt road of the highway.

"I wanna see that dragon!" yelled Mark.

"It's probably long gone by now," said Custer, holding onto the dash.

They followed the directions the GPS gave them, but they didn't need it, not with all the black smoke rising in the sky.

Mark slowed when they came upon the village. The mud huts burned, flames licking the sky, as if set on fire by a flame thrower and sprayed with accelerant.

"Watch out for fucking mines," said Custer, as Mark skidded to a stop. Custer turned to Brent. "Wizard? You're our sapper."

"Right," Brent said, and got out of the Bradley, staff first. As a "sapper," he knew he had to find any IED's in the vicinity. He could see piles of ash and pools of melted sand. He walked around to the front of the vehicle.

The spell in his mind flowed out through the staff. To his left, about a half a kilometer away, a mine exploded. Dust and dirt mixed with the ash and covered the pink and tan pools of sand. He walked to the village's main street and waved his hands over his head, signaling all clear. The Bradley followed his path and pulled up to him.

To make the fires stop, Brent knew he needed to deny the flames oxygen. He raised his staff and summoned the wind. It built up in front of him, pulling the flames with it. By the time the men got to him, he had a flaming tornado, about the size of a small Jeep, churning sand and ash in the funnel. The flames on the buildings fed the tornado, eaten up by the wind. He mentally pushed the tight tornado away from them, toward the opposite edge of the village.

Another mine exploded under it, the sand flowing into the vortex. Brent dispersed the spell and the tornado faded, flames disappearing among the dust, sand, and ash, floating into a pile on the ground. Brent leaned against the Bradley, panting. Wind and fire were not really in his repertoire.

Mark got out of the vehicle, and the rest cautiously followed.

"See if anything survived this," said Custer, hefting his gun. He said to Jason and Cory, "You two take the west, Mark and I'll take east. Wizard, you're center."

Brent slammed the base of his staff into the ground to get energy. The crystal on top glowed white for a moment, then faded quickly as Brent pulled the energy into him, ready for use. Brent watched the men separate. His military training kicked in so he hugged the walls, though they were still hot to the touch. He slowly made his way down the street, staff in the lead.

He felt it before he saw it: powerful magic. He looked up, stepping out to the center of the street.

Something flew toward the village. Something big and red. As it grew closer, he could see the wings.

"Holy shit," he muttered, and almost pissed his pants.

It came closer, easily bigger than an Apache helicopter. The huge red dragon flew right over the village, close enough to feel its passing above him. It landed gracefully, right beside the Bradley.

Brent, ignoring the possibility of any mines, ran up the center road to see Mark standing just past the Bradley. Custer approached the dragon speaking to it.

"... third infantry," he heard Custer say.

"Staff Sergeant Meghan Belliveau," said a woman's voice somewhere near the dragon.

Brent moved closer. The dragon looked like it could easily eat half their vehicle in one bite. Red and squat, it stood over two stories high. It resembled an enormous lizard, with wide tufts for ears, and teeth as big as a man's leg. Its legs were relatively short and thick; folded red wings took up most of the length of its body.

A female Marine in light kit sat on the neck of the dragon. She wore no helmet, which was against all the rules of the military, but carried a parachute on her back. She sat like a jockey, her knees up near her chest, the stirrups of the saddle set high. She looked comfortable there, and the dragon looked like it didn't even notice. Compared to the dragon, she was tiny, as big as one of its ears.

"Staff Sergeant," said Custer, "What brings you here?"

"Checking to make sure there were no survivors. Tyrath saw people moving here and came to investigate." She looked down at Brent, noticing his staff. "You're a wizard."

"Master Sergeant Brent Rogers," said Custer, introducing him.

"Sir," said the staff sergeant, saluting.

Brent returned it instinctively. The dragon rumbled. Brent looked at the dragon who looked at Brent as if contemplating swiping him with one of those evil claws.

"Tyrath doesn't like wizards, sir. My apologies."

Brent swallowed. *As long as it doesn't eat me.*

The Marine patted the dragon's neck. The dragon snorted, gray smoke rising from its nostrils.

Said Custer, "Mind looking around with us?"

"We can help, sir."

She leaned forward and said something to the dragon. The dragon raised its wings and jumped, kicking up a cloud of dirt not unlike a helicopter taking off. It gained some altitude, far enough away to see the entire village.

Mark grinned. "Did you see that? Did you fuckin' *see* that?"

Jason slapped Mark upside the back of his head. "Shut up, man."

"What I wouldn't give to ride on the back of that thing."

Jason shook his head. Cory kept looking up. Jason grabbed him and they began to explore the eastern side of the village.

Brent got through the first of two buildings on the street, when he heard a loud whoosh. The building next to him caught fire, the dragon hovering above it, wings fanning the flames. Brent dashed away from the burning building.

"Nothing left in there, sir!" called Belliveau.

The dragon seemed to grin, showing long, pointy teeth, then turned and flew north. Brent watched as the building melted, collapsing inward. He leaned hard against the second hut, gasping in the warm air. He forced himself to not hyperventilate.

I won't lose it. Not here.

The dragon landed at the northern collection of destroyed huts. It took a little while for everyone to assemble near it.

The dragon was a major distraction to the men — at least Cory and Mark. Mark grinned like a lunatic, inching his way closer to the beast. Cory hugged his gun and stared. The dragon turned to Mark and huffed at him, blowing black smoke in his direction. Mark backed off.

Custer gazed up past the dragon to its rider. "You can go now."

The Marine saluted. The dragon took three steps north, then launched into the air. He intentionally kicked up a pile of sand in their direction, like a cat covering its tracks.

"Shit," said Mark in wonder.

Brent turned from the men, the dragon, and the burned-out hulks of buildings. Brent couldn't bring himself to put out the last few remaining fires. The team stood by and watched them flame out, heading back to base at dusk.

2

KABUL

F OR THE TWO WEEKS until Combat Task Force Thunder got disbanded, Mark, unofficially, of course, chased the dragon. They didn't see the beast again, but they did see the destruction it left behind. Melted buildings sometimes turned into glass; piles of ash that could have been animals, articles, or people.

Brent didn't like these side excursions. They detracted from their missions of searching out Taliban. He always had a lump in his stomach whenever they approached a smoking ruin.

After CTF Thunder was terminated, the men travelled to Kabul for R&R and new orders. Kabul wasn't exactly cosmopolitan, but it was what passed for a city in Afghanistan.

Brent also headed to Kabul to get new orders at the Magic Corps, abbreviated Magicorps in military slang. He assumed he was going to be separated from the team, as his abilities were always in need somewhere. He would say his goodbyes in Kabul.

The journey would take them a full 24 hours, and they planned on driving all night. It started fine — no IED's on the well-travelled asphalt highway. It had been searched by sappers and engineers an hour or so before the convoy started.

Brent noticed a few stretches of highway perfect for an ambush. Buildings lined one side or another, or short brush with knobby trees and greenery. Fields of poppy and marijuana grew for miles.

About half an hour after Mark said, "It's too easy," they came to a stop. This wasn't good. Twenty kilometers to their left a field of poppies bloomed.

The radio crackled, "Truck One is down. Repeat: Truck One is down."

They heard the unmistakable thump of Rocket Propelled Grenades. Brent turned around in his seat to see a vehicle in the line list to the right, hanging off the road.

Then Brent heard the *whiz-ping* of bullets hitting the Bradley.

"Aw fuck," Mark said, as Custer opened the passenger door and dove out.

Since Brent was opposite the direction the bullets came from, he opened the back door for Jason, Cory. and himself to pile out.

"I'm gonna move Truck One out of the way," Brent yelled over the bullets.

Custer nodded, taking aim with his rifle over the hood of the Bradley. Brent made a quick decision.

He had learned a new spell while on leave: teleporting. He could pull his body into the spirit world that overlaid the real world and run to the next spot he needed to be in, then pull his body out of the spirit world. There were many problems with that spell — not the least of which was the spirit world was not an *exact* copy of the real world. In the spirit world, there may be nothing; in the real world, there may be a temporary object, and he could find himself teleported into the engine of a truck. Needless to say, that result did not end well for the magus. Instead, he decided to run the half-mile in the real world.

Brent ran behind the trucks, his shield spell up as he ran. He had learned to use his staff as a repository of a spell, so that the simple shield spell he knew could be put into the staff and run constantly.

The men of the convoy's first Humvee used the vehicle as cover to return fire into the poppy fields. Brent yelled to the sergeant, "I'll move this out of the way!"

The sergeant looked at Brent's staff, registering that he was a wizard. "Get it off the road."

Brent stood at the Humvee's passenger side. He raised his arms, the staff glowing with the shield spell, and the vehicle rose a foot or so off the ground. He pushed it toward the poppy fields, clearly out of the way of the Humvee behind it. The men used it as cover, hiding and shooting as the truck moved closer to the fields.

The Humvee next to them crawled forward on the highway. Truck Two slowly inched between him and the truck, causing his spell to collapse because the truck wasn't in his line of sight. Truck Three followed, its driver hunkered down even though the driver's side window was bullet-proof.

Brent watched the vehicles pass by. As soon as the trucks started moving, the gunfire slowed down, then stopped completely.

"Can you carry this back to Kabul?" the sergeant asked Brent.

"Are you kidding?"

"Thought you wizards can do anything."

Then, Brent saw his team's Bradley come trundling down the road. He smiled and stepped out to meet them.

Mark wasn't his usual smiling self. He opened the window to talk to Brent. "Cory," he said.

Brent's smile faded. "Is he injured?" Even though Cory didn't like Brent's sorcery, he felt obligated to help him.

"He's dead," said Mark. "Stupid cherry move."

Cory must have stood up and made himself a target. Brent normally protected the young man when he stood to fire.

"Shit," said Brent. Although he was a healer, he wasn't a necromancer, and couldn't raise people from the dead.

Custer looked around Mark's bulk to say, "We'll take care of him. You'd better stay here in case they need help with the wrecker."

Brent nodded. He looked at Mark, obviously sad.

Mark said, "We have to bring him home."

"Yeah, I know. I'll stay here."

Mark nodded. "See ya."

He cranked the window shut, and a sense of finality swept over Brent. He would never see these men again. The Bradley pulled away, as he stared at the back door, with Cory inside. Brent sighed as another truck drove by, blocking his view.

Brent dismounted the wrecker at Camp Phoenix in Kabul, heading directly to Magic Corps HQ. Over the door of the building hung a picture of their patch: a wand with stars over it. He pushed open the door and smelled magic.

Some magi had a scent to them. He smelled fresh grass on a dew-kissed morning. Underneath that aroma was a deep, earthy smell that seemed to go right to his animal brain to make him sniff for more. Mulch? Patchouli? Something like that.

He went down the small corridor and reached a woman at the end of the hallway.

"Cybalia."

A woman in an Army-issue tan uniform sat at a desk. Tanned dark, she had the coloring of an Afghan woman. However, she was a clairvoyant of the Army. Her black eyes looked up at Brent.

"We have been expecting you. Please go right in."

Brent opened the plywood door and entered the study of Archmage Henry Dieter. Brent closed the door and saluted.

"At ease, Master Sergeant," said the archmage.

Tall, fit, with white hair — supposedly from too much death magic — Dieter had a chiseled face, clean-shaven, the hair cut in an Army crew. His bright blue eyes watched him over a pair of wire-frame glasses.

Brent stood at parade rest. "I am here for new orders, sir."

"Good. We need a liaison for the Marine Fifth Wing. They're in Kunar Province."

"A liaison? Sir, diplomacy is not my strongest suit."

"Make it one." He tucked a hand into a drawer, pulling out a packet with his orders. "We already have one there, but he's needed elsewhere. You need to maintain a healthy distance between the Fifth Wing and the Army. Remember who you work for."

Brent noticed that he had gone rigid. He forced himself to relax.

"You have your orders. Leave right now and you'll get a bird to FOB Blessing."

"Yes, sir," said Brent, saluting.

He left the office, thinking, *Why the Marines?*

3

FOB BLESSING, KUNAR PROVINCE

BRENT HITCHED A RIDE out to the airfield, looking for Marines. They were hard to find, shoehorned in among the Army. He could pick out the Army easily, as some still wore green items with their tan uniforms. He finally found an Osprey loading up supplies, heading for Kunar Province. They were going to Aslamabad. From there, he could ride with the transport or get another bird to Forward Operating Base Blessing.

When he got to Aslamabad airfield, he arrived minutes before a helicopter left for FOB Blessing. He squeezed into the back of an Apache, wondering if the archmage did a spell or if it was all coincidence. Brent didn't think it was the latter.

"What brings you here?" asked the helo pilot through the headset that Brent had to wear.

"New orders," said Brent. "I'm supposed to be a liaison."

"Between who?"

"Fifth Wing and the Army."

The men chuckled. "Good luck with that," said the copilot. "You gotta kiss their asses so they go on missions."

"And hope they don't blow up shit while they're out there," said another man.

"Aren't they Marines?" asked Brent. That kind of behavior was not tolerated in the Marine Corps.

"Only in name," said the pilot. "They were here before most of us."

Brent had heard rumors that the Marines and some special forces teams had come to Afghanistan days after 9/11. Maybe the Fifth Wing consisted of special forces of Marines and *mujahideen* — leftovers from the Soviet era.

Brent mulled on that as the deafening sound of the helicopter gave him a thumping headache.

Forward Operating Base Blessing had the worst placement, located between the base of some mountains, and the banks of a river. A beautiful place to build a resort, but horrible to put a military camp. Taliban and other insurgents could easily fire into the base, and they did so with a great amount of frequency. There were a few Gansett metal containers set up in rows as their barracks.

"All out," said the pilot as he landed in the northern part of the base.

The rotors slowed, taking their own sweet time stopping. Here, as back in Kabul, the Marines mixed in with the Army, though he noticed they didn't meld well with each other. The Marines talked to his stripes and not to him. One of the Marines guided him directly to the central office.

Although not the CO, Army Major Josephson sat behind a desk placed in an area no bigger than a walk-in closet. A portable air conditioner, the desk, a chair before the desk, and a small refrigerator completed the setup.

After salutes, Brent explained his orders. "Good luck with that, Master Sergeant."

"The Fifth Wing seems to have a reputation."

"Oh, they do. Not the jockeys, but the mounts. They bite the hand that feeds them."

Brent furrowed his brow. He felt the tightness of his face showing confusion. "Mounts?"

The major said, "You mean you don't know?"

"I'm sorry, I don't know."

"The Fifth Wing consists of four dragons."

Brent staggered like he got sucker-punched.

The major started to get up. "You okay?"

Brent broke out into a cold sweat. He couldn't breathe. He saw the chair and dropped into it. The major got a bottled water out of the refrigerator. Brent twisted the cap and drank it like a man lost for months in the desert. He used the moment to calm his racing mind using techniques learned from the Magic Corps.

The major waited, put a hand on Brent's shoulder. "I thought you knew."

Brent shook his head. *Communication in the Army*, he thought. *Don't tell them anything.* "I didn't know." He finished the water. "Sorry about that, sir."

"Never saw a man act that way about the dragons. Usually they're excited."

"I had a past experience concerning them." He handed the empty bottle to the major who tossed it at the wastebasket near the door. He missed. "Where are they?"

"There's a tent at the airfield. You'll find them there. The riders are in the container near the first aid station."

Brent got up. "I'll see the dragons first." *Might as well get that over with.*

"I'll send Lieutenant Waters to you."

"Who's he?"

"He's the present liaison between the TOC and the Fifth Wing. Unofficially, of course. The mounts are named Tyrath, Olron, Baldar, and Makrah. Makrah's the leader."

"Tyrath. I met him and his rider."

"Those two are the most difficult to manage. You'll see."

Brent headed out to the airfield. He found a container and a large tent adjacent to it. Relaxing on rugs outside of the tent, as if enjoying a pleasant evening, sat three men.

All of them were bare-chested, in cut-off uniform shorts, and barefoot. One had long curly black hair that fell past his shoulders in a thick braid, ending at the center of his chest. Another had shoulder-length black hair and said something to the first man as Brent began to approach. The third man had hair as white as phosphorous fire and smoked a hookah. As Brent got closer, the sun dipped behind the mountains, sending the area into shadow.

Where are the dragons?

The two black-haired men rose when Brent came into their circle. All three men had slanted cat's eyes: the white-haired man had dark blue eyes like the early dawn, the braided man had gold eyes, while the last man had eyes of emerald.

"Do you speak English?" Brent asked.

"What do you want, Magus?" asked the man with green eyes. His voice was half-rumble, half-growl, with a lilting accent that Brent couldn't place. He said his "g" in Magus as a soft "g", not *May-jus* as most people would say.

Brent looked at each one of the men in turn. "I'm looking for the Fifth Wing."

"Yes," said the man, "That's us."

"You're the riders?"

The blue-eyed stoner said, "We are the dragons." He gave Brent's stare right back at him.

Brent gathered himself and asked, "Who's your leader?"

The two black-haired men looked at the white-haired man smoking the hookah. They were kidding, right? This stoner was their leader?

"I am Makrah," said the man.

"Master Sergeant Brent Rogers." He offered his hand.

Makrah stared down at the hand, and then focused again on Brent's face. "What do you want?"

Brent pulled back his hand. The three dragons stared without blinking at him. The first speaker had crossed his arms. Brent thought back to when Custer had to establish connections with the villagers.

Be honest, up front, and don't let them tell you what to do.

"I am your liaison."

Said the first speaker, "We already have one of those."

"He's needed elsewhere."

"We like Lieutenant Waters."

This is going to be harder than I thought. The man with the braid said nothing so far, but he had a knowing grin as he stared at Brent.

"I'm sorry, but that's the way the Army goes. Have you ever been in the Army?"

"No," said the long-haired man, but Makrah said, "Yes." Makrah continued, "We do not want a new ... liaison."

Brent heard the crunch of sand behind him and turned around to see an Army man carrying a box coming their way. He hesitated for a moment at seeing Brent.

"Lieutenant Waters," called the short-haired man. "This man is taking your place."

The lieutenant was just over Brent's age, probably 30, with brown hair cut regulation short. He wore the typical Army uniform, tan colored, complete with cap and a Magic Corps wand patch on his left arm.

"Hello," he said, setting the box down on one of the rugs.

Now the braided-man moved and opened the box. Inside it lay four large hunks of raw meat wrapped in plastic. They looked like they came from cattle, the legs still attached. The braided man took one of the bundles and retreated to a rug away from them. He sat down cross-legged and tore open the plastic.

"Who are you?" demanded Waters.

"Master Sergeant Brent Rogers. I'm relieving you of duty."

"Relieving me? Why?"

"You should be getting new orders soon."

Makrah took one of the bundles of raw meat as Brent heard a distinct *crunch* from the area where the braided man sat down. He refused to look.

He grabbed Brent by the arm and pulled him a short distance away, saying, "You have no idea what I had to do to get these guys to do what I want."

"I've been told to relieve you. You can bump it up the chain."

"They're the Marines' Fifth Wing. You're in the Army. You can't tell them what to do."

"You're in the Army, too, Lieutenant. I have my orders."

Waters said coldly, "We'll have to see about that, *Sergeant.*"

He turned and went back to the three dragons, all of whom were sitting down and eating the raw meat — bones and all. Brent screwed up his courage and walked back to them.

The man with the braid eyed Brent as if he was dessert. Makrah drank from a canteen to wash down the raw meat, while the long-haired man sucked the marrow from the bones.

"You will rectify this situation," said Makrah, looking at Waters. "We do not need anyone new."

"Of course, my lord," said Waters. Brent gave him a surprised look. "I'm sure this is all a misunderstanding by Command."

Said the braided man, "Maybe he is here for a snack." He had a Russian accent. The other two dragons chuckled. Brent stood his ground.

"Where is Baldar?" asked Waters.

"Wherever there is air conditioning," said the long-haired man, crunching the bones.

"I can't keep this here. It'll rot."

"I will take it," said the Russian.

"You will eat it, Tyrath," said Makrah. "I will hold it."

Tyrath? Brent said, "You're the dragon I saw in Nangahar Province."

The man grinned. He had more teeth than was possible for a human. "I remember you, Magus. I very much remember you."

Makrah, Waters, and the other dragon, probably Olron, scowled at Brent.

Brent stood up straighter. "I'm going to talk to the riders. Let them know if they need anything for you, they have to go through me."

"I will be talking to command about this," said Waters.

"You do just that." Brent turned, parade-style, and stormed with his staff to the container next to the tent.

Two Gansett containers stood about fifty feet away from the dragon's tent. Rounded roofs at the top to keep off the elements, they sat like twin elongated silver half-moons in the lush valley. A red cross decorated the container closest to the airfield. The other had no insignia.

Inside the plain one, he smelled rust and sweat, gun oil and cigarette smoke. The barracks here probably held the pilots and airmen of the helicopters that ran shuttle from Blessing to all points. He could hear snoring through some of the open doors that let some of the air conditioning pump through. He walked down the corridor, peering into rooms. Then he saw one door with a sheet of paper taped on it: a hand-drawn red heraldic dragon, sitting on its hind legs with his front paw up. Brent knocked on the flimsy door.

A young woman opened it. Her long brown hair was pulled up in a ponytail. She wore a Marine t-shirt and shorts and was barefoot like the dragons. She looked familiar.

"I know you."

"Yes, sir." She saluted. "Sergeant Belliveau. We met with Tyrath."

He returned the salute. "I'm looking for the dragon riders."

"Come on in."

The woman stepped aside for Brent.

Two other women sat on the bunks in the room. One stood up. "I'm Debbie. This is Jen." Debbie pointed to another woman sitting on a bed. Both had their hair cut very short, not quite a jarhead, but certainly within regulations. They all saluted him.

"There are four dragons, yes?" asked Brent.

"Shorty's with the guys playing video games or something," said Jen, who returned to sitting cross-legged on the cot.

"I'll go find her later."

"Him."

"Right. Him. I just wanted to let you know that I'm going to be the liaison between the dragons and the Armed Forces."

"Waters must love that," said Meghan. "He's their lackey."

He turned to her. "Tell me about Tyrath."

Meghan shrugged. "What do you want to know?"

"How long have you been working with Tyrath?"

"Three months and two days."

"And who destroys the villages?"

She looked up at him. "Sir?"

"Do you order Tyrath to destroy any villages?"

"What — no, sir!"

"You're his rider, I take it?"

"Yes, sir."

"Don't you control him?"

Her mouth broke into a grin, just short of a laugh. "Sir, we're their riders so they don't destroy friendlies."

"How do you know what to do? Do you have radios?"

Meghan said, "We stop the patrol near a command post and get orders from the ground. I'm sure they need breaks, and so do we."

"How did you get to work with Tyrath?"

"They were looking for small, light-weight riders. We three girls fit the bill."

"Okay," said Brent, leaning on his staff. "Who and where is Baldar?"

"He sometimes hangs out with Shorty. He sits under the air conditioning."

"Why does he do that?"

"He's a frost dragon."

Oh, that explains it. So not all the dragons are fire and brimstone.

Brent heard a loud thump from outside and jumped.

Mortars from outside the base.

He knew they couldn't get him in here, so he continued, "I'm going to find your orders for tomorrow and I'll probably see you off in the morning."

"Yes, sir," they all said.

He started to leave, then paused. "Any place I can sleep?"

"Down the hall are some cots," said Jen. "You'll have to leave the door open, though or you'll suffocate."

"Okay, thanks. I'll see you all tomorrow, then." After salutes, he left the room.

Brent walked down the corridor to its end. He tried the last room on the left. It opened into a dark, lightless room. He tried to find a light switch on the wall, but didn't feel any.

Brent summoned a mage light — a small ball of floating electricity from his essence. The wan white light illuminated a room with six sturdy bunk beds. The air conditioning wasn't very strong here, but at least the sound of the mortars were distant muffled thumps.

Four dragons. One a stoner. One a Russian. One Brent hadn't met. And one he wasn't sure about. And the present liaison was an asshole.

He heard Scar's voice as soon as he closed his eyes. "The dragons."

He felt his heart race, his shoulder throb. He was instantly back in the freezer, hanging by his wrists, his shoulder pierced.

"I don't know."

Brent felt the hit in his gut by an invisible force. Scar repeated, "The dragons. There are four."

"I just met them! I don't know anything!"

"You will find out, Sergeant Rogers. And you will tell me *everything*."

He clawed his way out of the nightmare, opening his eyes in the gloom. He was covered in sweat, shaking. He couldn't concentrate to summon a mage light.

He breathed, slow and deep. The phantom pain in his shoulder faded as he closed eyes again. He consciously pulled Chrissie into his mind's eye. "I have to call you, hun," he said quietly before drifting into a slightly more restful sleep.

4

KUNAR PROVINCE

T HE DRAGONS WERE much more formidable at full size.
Brent thought he could tell each one of them by their size and color. A cobalt blue worm-like dragon with wide webbed feet lay in the early morning dimness.

Another cornflower-colored dragon with silver armor across its chest sat on its haunches at the foot of the mountain. Brent assumed that was Makrah because of the armor. Even sitting like a cat with its long reptilian tail curled around its front claws, he was easily twenty feet tall.

In comparison, Tyrath stood like a lizard on four short legs, his wings spread wide. Meghan sat comfortably on the back of his neck, just behind the huge tufts of his ears.

The last dragon looked, to Brent, like a dragon should. Thin and elegant, he had red scales, with some along his wings that were of a lighter, rust color. The worm dragon eyed Brent and turned to face him. Brent couldn't read dragons' emotions on their faces, so he didn't know what was going through their minds.

Brent watched as two Marines swarmed over each dragon, putting on the saddles. The riders, wearing fatigues, with parachutes on their backs and their vests full of water bottles, used ropes to climb up into the saddles. Shorty, a relatively small Marine who seemed packed of solid muscle, climbed onto the blue worm dragon's neck, right behind his head.

The riders didn't have a radio, so Brent understood why they had to stop to retrieve orders. Brent, at three in the morning, had stopped by HQ and gotten the dragons' orders for now.

Makrah and Olron were a "show of force." They would fly north, show themselves and make a lot of noise. Tyrath, flying south among mountain passes, would report on any smugglers that he could find. Brent was going to follow Baldar, who had a village in the west he was going to visit, as a backup to a patrol in a village with Marines.

As the armored dragon flew up in the air, his rider firmly on his back, Brent marveled at the magnificence of the beasts. Although huge on the ground, in moments, they disappeared into the early morning sky.

Brent jumped into the helicopter with the Marines as they headed to the village of Walif. Allegedly some radio chatter came from there talking about a smuggler in town, who the Marines called Jackdaw.

They flew out into the desert. After a fifteen-minute flight, they were deposited a couple of kilometers west of Walif. The town was a cluster of houses with an orchard on the east side.

The early morning stars were their only light. They didn't need the night vision goggles with the starlight.

The Marines trooped single-file through the desert to a small hill near the village — confident, but very careful. Still early, the Marines were to meet up with some members of the Afghan Army. They hadn't shown up at the rendezvous point yet.

Dawn came with only Venus, the morning star, remaining in the sky. Still no Afghan army. The sergeant in charge of the platoon radioed back to base, sounding calm but venting to the men around him.

In the village after dawn. people came out of houses, women feeding animals, young boys herding goats or skinny cows. The goats reminded Brent of the dragons, who subsided on raw meat. Where was he going to find butchered animals? Waters probably wouldn't be forthcoming about it.

Someone said, "Fuck, we've been spotted."

A Marine with a pair of binoculars sat below the crest of the hill, observing the town outskirts A woman looked out in their direction.

"We'll have to go in *now*," said the leader of the platoon, a Sergeant Meyers, who also radioed that in.

As the Marines entered the village, people and children walked around them. To Brent, this meant the Taliban probably didn't use this village as a staging area — yet. At a small bazaar, people looked over food and clothing. The Marines seemed to be wary. Brent took out the translation stone to overhear the conversations.

"You son of a dog, you expect me to pay how much for that?"

"These men look ready for a fight."

"Occupiers."

"Fashim, better tell Kaliss infidels are here."

The leader of the platoon listened to the radio for a minute. "Jackdaw's here," he said. "We need to find out who he is."

Brent stepped back as the Marines walked deeper into town. The Marines had no translator, so had to rely on body language alone to convey who was friendly. Brent knew that nervous people were not indicative of friendlies. He walked over to a market stall of fabric and examined the wares without touching them. He kept his hands loose at his sides, holding the stone.

The stall owner said, smiling, "Hey, idiot soldier. Buy one of my *hajib* for your slutty girlfriend."

"No, thank you," said Brent also smiling.

The man paled. "You speak Pashtun?"

"Enough," Brent said with a shrug.

"I-I-I am sorry, friend. Please, please, take this as an offer of apology." He picked up a long piece of red material threaded with gold, easily the most expensive item he had. Instead, Brent pointed to a simple black and white commercially patterned man's scarf.

The man picked it out of his wares. "I do humbly apologize."

Brent took it, carefully folding it into his pack. "Do you know of any Taliban here?"

He looked horrified that he was asked such a question.

Brent expected an answer like that. He kept his voice low. "I know that if you did, you wouldn't say so at peril to your life. But as it's the scorpion's habit to sting, it's my habit to ask."

The man smiled and nodded.

Brent leaned forward, as if he was examining some material closely. "Where is the radio?" Brent asked, just above a whisper.

The man got the hint and leaned forward also. "Second road on the left." He glared at Brent. "That one, I'm afraid you'll have to pay for."

"How much?"

"Ten American."

Brent tucked into his pocket and pulled out his wallet, sliding out a ten. He knew Afghans preferred US dollars to the Afghani. This man was taking a chance using US dollars, though. If the Taliban caught him with US dollars, he would probably be put to death. He also knew that Afghans liked to haggle, and Americans usually didn't, so he fulfilled the stereotype and got the baby blue *hajib* for its asking price. It would be a curiosity for Chrissie. The dealer took the money and put it in his pocket.

"Thank you," said Brent. He saw three Marines watching him. He didn't see the rest of the platoon.

Brent jogged up to the three Marines. "I got a lead."

The three men looked at each other. "Sarge," one called on the radio.

Dropping the translation stone in his pocket, Brent said to Sergeant Meyers, "I got a lead, sir."

The sergeant nodded, looked to the three Marines. He spoke to two of them: "Granger, Lamb, go with the wizard."

Granger reminded Brent a lot of Cody. Lamb was a blond, blue-eyed juggernaut that made his sniper rifle look like a toy in his hands.

Brent beckoned and the men followed. They walked down an alley and at the second intersection, he stopped. There were three houses on this "street". The house at the end had very young, half-naked children playing chase in the dirt in front; the other two looked unoccupied.

"Jackdaw's in one of these houses," Brent said.

The men headed to the last house. Granger went up to the kids. Lamb tried to look intimidating, which wasn't hard.

Brent took the stone and asked the kids, "Where are your parents?"

A couple of kids shrugged. Either they didn't know or didn't understand. One of the others glanced at the house before shrugging also.

Granger walked over to the house and knocked. "US Army," he said in Pashtun. "Open up!"

They heard movement. Then something thudded inside the house.

"Back door!" yelled Lamb, running around. Granger almost went through the front door, but instead went around the other side to the back.

Brent rounded the corner to see two men heading at full tilt toward the orchard, about fifty meters from the town. They had a good head start, and, with the Marines laden with packs, they probably could get away. Not for lack of trying, the two Marines ran, dust puffing off them as they chased the two men.

The roar of the dragon made the hair on Brent arm stand on end. The dragon swooped down, the sunlight glinting off his silver armor. He exhaled snow and ice on the orchard, creating a wall of ice. The Afghan men tried to stop, but slipped and slid into the ice wall, landing ignominiously with their butts up in the air. Granger and Lamb got to them. While slipping and sliding on the ice, they pulled the two men to their feet.

In the meantime, Sergeant Meyers arrived. Granger and Lamb patted down the Afghan men, with Granger putting something away. Brent looked up in the sky to see the dragon had gone back to circling the area.

How did he see from all the way up there? Brent wondered.

Granger and Lamb pushed the men forward, making them walk back to the house where the rest of the platoon waited. Meyers said, "Fuck, I need a translator."

Brent held out the translation stone. "Use this. Just hold it in your left hand. You'll be able to understand what they say, and they'll understand you no matter what language you speak."

The Marine looked at the stone as if it was a live grenade. "You sure?"

"I use it all the time."

He took the stone, clenching it tightly in his fist.

The two captured men wore typical Afghan dress. One tanned man wore a knee-length black vest and dirty white tunic; the other, equally tanned, wore a distinctive dirty blue scarf and grey turban.

Granger and Lamb stepped up and tossed three items on the ground: an AK-47 and two Russian pistols. Meyers nodded approvingly at the two soldiers.

Brent sat on the back stairs of the building they had chased the men from. Placing his staff across his knees, he watched the interrogation. First, they separated the two men.

"We're going to look in that house," said Meyers. "And if we find a radio and you've been lying to us, you'll be in a hell of a lot of trouble."

The man shrugged. Afghans did this as a rule. When confronted with evidence, they would shrug and come up with a story. Brent could force them to tell the truth. He had spells for that and, augmented with his knack, he could interrogate easily. But it would make him sick and out of sorts, so he didn't want to do it. Besides, in Brent's opinion, Meyers had been doing fine up to that point.

"Let's check out the house, Sarge," said one of the Marines.

Brent got up from the steps, expecting them to do just that.

Instead, Meyers kept questioning the man with the blue scarf, "What's in the fucking house? Are we gonna walk into a fucking ambush?"

Brent sighed as the man clammed up. He turned to face the door. "Better get the kids out of the front," he said.

One of the Marines turned to Brent, then back to Meyers. "What's up, Wizard?"

"A feeling."

"Well, motherfuckers? Is there a fucking bomb in there?" Meyers leaned forward to intimidate the two Afghans.

"Allow me to look," said Brent. Even though Brent technically outranked the sergeant, he still asked permission out of courtesy. Plus, he was outnumbered by at least six burly Marines.

"Yeah," said Meyers.

Brent put a hand on the door and whispered the seeing spell. He closed his eyes and, in his mind's eye, could see the inside of the room. "There's ammo against the right wall, behind the door," Brent said. "RPG's and rockets, boxes of ammo." He scanned the room, the ceiling, and through a doorway into the front room, "In the other room is a grenade. It looks like a dud, sir."

"Russian-made bullshit," said Meyers.

"Sir," said the Marine, "Let me go first."

"Be careful," said Brent. There were rugs strewn about, probably hiding IED's. Brent summoned a bright mage light which followed the man into the room, throwing light into the corners. "And under that rug is an IED."

"Fuck, man," said a man following the Marine. "Why don't all the patrols have a guy like this?"

"Cuz then we'd get lazy, mother fucker," said a big black man. He gave Brent an evil eye.

Brent shrugged it off and stepped back outside. "Get the ordinance," said Meyers, "and radio the ANP to arrest these two."

The men searched among the rooms, taking out many boxes of ammo, grenades, missile launchers, mortars, and guns. Some were American-made but most were Russian — a small, but varied cache.

"These look new," said Meyers, opening some of the Russian boxes to find machine guns and bandoleers of bullets. "Which one of you is the radio operator?" he demanded of the two men.

Again, they shrugged.

The sergeant handed the stone back to Brent, happy to be rid of it. "We're not going to get any more out of these two."

A crowd of people had gathered by now. Out of that group, five men in a mixture of black, green, and tan uniforms casually pushed their way through the crowd.

"Finally," said Meyers, approaching them. "Where were you?"

"We were waiting," said a man, and pointed to the orchard. "We did not see you. We heard the dragon and saw the ice."

"Took you long enough," muttered one of the men.

Meyers ignored the jibe. "See these guys? One of them is the one we're looking for."

"We spoke with the elders," said the ANA soldier. "They want to see these men."

"Why?" The sergeant pointed to the cache. "It's pretty obvious what they were doing."

"The elders will say so."

"Jesus Christ, are they fucking kidding?" said Granger.

Meyers glared at the two prisoners. The ANA men flanked the two civilians and guided them through the crowd.

"What're we gonna do with this shit?" asked Lamb.

"Take it with us." Meyers turned to the Marine radio operator. "Get us a truck to load this shit."

As they waited for the truck, the crowd dispersed. Brent saw the market stall seller who had given him the information. The seller glared hatefully at Brent, then turned away. Brent wasn't sure if it was for show or real, but he washed his face of emotion to not give anything away.

The five ANA men never returned with the prisoners.

Brent didn't hear about Tyrath until he got back to base. Another large village in Kandahar Province had been nuked. The elections in the area would have been held there in October.

Brent got out of his kit and put on a t-shirt, tunic, and pants, and headed back out. As he waited for the dragons to return, he tried to stay out of the way of the men working on the helicopters. He perched himself on a crate and watched the shimmering sky.

A man casually came up to him. His brown hair was cut to stubble like most of the Marines out there. He looked like cinder blocks piled in a square, set on long thick legs. His t-shirt clung to him, a little too tightly, as he possibly had filled it out while working.

"Need me to move?" Brent asked.

"No, sir," said the man in a light Southern voice. "You're fine." He turned in the direction Brent was looking. "Waitin' on a bird?"

"Fifth Wing."

"Ah, those dragons. Ever talk to 'em?"

"Just a little last night."

Looking out at the sky, the man said, "They don' much like the Children of the Moon."

Brent took stock of the man. He wasn't a vampire — it was too bright out here for one. He might have been fae, but he wasn't delicate enough. "Lucan?"

"Yup." DADT, Don't-Ask-Don't-Tell, extended to Children of the Moon. They could be treated differently if people knew.

"Where you from?"

"Texas. You?"

"Massachusetts."

"You ain't got that Boston accent."

"I'm from Worcester, not Boston."

"We got counties bigger than your state."

Brent chuckled. He held out his hand. "Brent."

"Kurt," said the man, engulfing Brent's hand in his own. They shook firmly, briefly testing each other's mettle.

"You ain't gonna say nothing, are you?"

"Not my place." Brent said. "I'm just a magus."

"Don't you guys come after us if we fuck up?"

"Me? Keep the Children in line? That's *way* above my pay grade."

"They make it sound like it in Basic."

"Maybe they do that to make the grunts feel better."

"And keep us scared of y'all."

Brent shrugged. "You with the K9, too?"

"Every full moon." Kurt perked his head up. "Something's coming in."

Brent couldn't see it. In a few minutes, though, he did see a speck in the distance.

"I'd better get back before Sarge sends a posse out on my ass."

"Be seeing you, Kurt."

Kurt waved and Brent watched him go. Brent looked back at the large speck getting larger. It was the worm-like dragon.

Brent got down off the crate to head to the tent.

★　　★　　★

"Makrah!" Brent called to the white-haired man. "Thank you for helping the Marines earlier today."

Makrah paused. "I did nothing."

"You're not the blue dragon with the armor?"

"That is not me. That is Baldar. Where is Waters?"

"I don't know. I've been out."

"Waters is to bring us food."

"You should eat what we eat."

"Your 'chow' makes us sick. Olron goes there. He may be there now." Makrah glared at Brent. "If you do not have meat, why are you here?"

"I'm looking for Tyrath."

"He is with Meghan."

"Do you know —"

"They are probably busy. They do not want to be disturbed while mating."

Brent blinked. "While what?"

"The woman wants to mate." Makrah shrugged.

Brent felt his face grow hot as he pictured the two of them in his mind's eye. "She should know better than that. Jesus." Brent started toward the tent. "Are they in here?"

"No."

"Fuck," Brent spat, staring at the tent, his mind racing.

"Is this another rule?"

"What do you mean?"

"The armies have many rules. We cannot mate with your women?"

"Yes. You cannot mate with the women."

"What about the men?"

Brent almost burst out in an uncomfortable laugh. "No, not the men, either."

Makrah stood back, his hands behind his back. "How unfortunate. It is good to mate before battle."

"Can he get her pregnant?"

"We are dragons. Unless the woman can create us, then no." Makrah looked beyond Brent. "Baldar."

Brent turned around to see a bald man wearing only a pair of pants, his skin tinged blue by the twilight. He had one solid block of abs instead of six distinctive squares. His blue eyes bored into Brent like a pair of picks.

"The magus," he said, his voice higher-pitched than the other dragons. "I heard about you."

Baldar turned to Makrah and spat something in a severe language that sounded like German and Russian combined. He walked by Brent and into the tent.

"What was that all about?"

"He called you a whelp. Which is amusing coming from one." Makrah shrugged. "Baldar is a frost dragon. This weather makes him grumpy."

"I heard that!" came Baldar's voice from the tent.

Makrah said to Brent. "Get us our food."

Brent said, "You get me Tyrath."

"Agreed."

On the way to mess, Brent saw Olron, wearing only a pair of regulation boxers, standing in the sunny side of one of the containers. Like most of the men, he didn't seem embarrassed. He carried a pair of Army issue camo shorts. He saw Brent and paused.

Just seeing the man in the sun, Brent couldn't understand how he could stand the heat.

He's a fire dragon, Brent thought. *He probably lives in a lava lake somewhere.*

"Hi, Olron."

"Wizard! I heard you were with Baldar today."

"He didn't stick around."

"He doesn't like the desert. He prefers night missions. And he'd rather be in the mountains, but he doesn't want to go alone."

"The Northern mountains aren't that far. I can talk to the CO."

Olron stepped into the camo shorts. "If he had his way, he'd be in a crystal ice cave somewhere with his GI Joe action figures."

Brent blinked. "His what?"

Olron laughed. "Dragons are classic hoarders, you know."

"I didn't know that."

"We all have collections. If you have a part of our collection, you can control us."

"So if I collect — I don't know —"

"Salt and pepper shakers from the fifty states."

"Seriously? Do you?"

"No," Olron laughed.

"If you did, and I had one ..."

"An original. Never seen anywhere else."

"I'd own you?"

"Yes."

"Does Waters have GI Joe figures?"

Olron laughed. "You're *all* the originals!"

"Does that mean ..."

Olron waited.

"We all own him?"

"That answer, only Baldar knows. But it's like your magical name. Not something we give out."

"You just told me Baldar's weakness."

He shrugged. "Fire and ice don't get along."

"By the way, how old are you?"

"In your years, I'm young. Only 320 years, as far as I can reckon."

"Are you a whelp?"

"Baldar is the whelp. He is only 200 years old."

Brent calculated. They were making dragons in the early 1700's? He wondered if the American Revolution — or even the Civil War — could have had dragons. What kind of destruction would there be?

Olron asked, "What's wrong?"

"You're not that old at all. How did you come to this world?"

"I don't know. We don't know. We ask that question among ourselves like you ask among yourselves. Most of us woke up here. Some of us — very few of us — learned at the feet of a magus."

"Rogers!"

Brent saw Waters storming toward him. His face was red, his body rigid.

"Uh oh," muttered Olron

"Lieutenant," said Brent, saluting him, but doing an intentionally sloppy job of it.

"What the fuck are you doing here?"

"I'm heading to chow to —"

"You're supposed to be at the TOC to meet with the commanders for a debriefing." He stabbed a finger at the watch on his wrist. "Every fucking day, at this fucking time."

"Well, Lieutenant, if you had told me instead of walking off last night —"

"Don't fucking blame me, magus." He got in Brent's face. "You and me, magus. We'll see who's better for these dragons."

"Are you challenging me?"

"Damn right."

Brent felt the old fire in his belly — the one he thought the Black Lions had beaten out of him. He grinned. "I would be most honored to have a duel," he said formally.

"Tomorrow. 0200."

"You're on."

Waters turned on his heel and marched away. Brent stared hard at the man's back, spells of destruction dancing through his mind. When Waters ducked around a corner, out of his line of sight, Brent took a deep breath to clear his mind and turned to Olron.

He was gone.

Brent turned around in a complete circle looking for him. He glanced back toward the dragons' tent, but no one was outside. He then headed to chow without any further interruptions.

When he got there, three burly Marines stood over a seated. smaller Olron. The Marines had their kits still on, and none of them looked happy. Brent saw a large piece of raw roast on Olron's plate.

"Obviously," said Olron in a condescending tone, "you haven't gotten the memo."

"Fuck the fuckin' memo — how come you get steak an' we get shit?"

Brent went over to the small group. "Excuse me," he said.

But before they looked at him, one of the Marines went to grab the roast.

Olron bit him.

His teeth were sharp, pointed, and not human. He bit so hard he crunched bone. The Marine howled as Olron tore the flesh from the man's arm, tearing the ulna out and snapping it in two. With the bone and flesh in his mouth, Olron chewed and swallowed.

Brent fought back nausea. The man with the injured arm moaned and stumbled back, biting his lip to stop himself from screaming. The two remaining Marines backed away.

"Fuck me," said one, and ran out the door.

The remaining Marine grabbed his injured friend and hustled him out.

"Jesus Christ," said Brent quietly. Louder, he berated Olron. "Did you have to do that?"

"I haven't had fresh meat in a while. It was tasty."

Brent swallowed. The nausea was close, really close.

Olron took the large roast and both hands and bit off a chunk. "It's horse meat," he said.

Brent tried to summon up a hot glare, but watching the dragon eat made his stomach flip. He knew the look on his face wasn't angry enough.

"We'll settle this later,' said Brent. "I have a healing to do."

Olron looked up, his face questioning, but Brent turned away from him without another word.

Brent made his way in the growing dark to the official hospital tent. Inside, he saw the Marine in a chair, his bleeding arm on a desk, getting it cleaned out. He wasn't howling now, taking it stoically.

Just like a Marine, Brent thought.

"You should realize," said the doctor, "That they're like wild animals."

"Nobody, "said the dark-skinned Marine, "nobody told me shit about fuckin' *dragons*."

"Well, now you know." The doctor looked up to see Brent. "I'll be with you in a moment."

"I've come to offer my assistance. I'm a magus."

The Marine looked up at Brent. "You're a fuckin' wizard?"

"Yes."

The Marine let out a short screech. The doctor sat back. "I've cleaned it. You can do your thing." He motioned to Brent.

The Marine said, "Will it hurt?"

"I'll try not to," said Brent, stepping over to the soldier. He'd seen worse before, though he tried not to picture the dragon swallowing the man's flesh. He placed his hand on the crook of the man's elbow. "What's your name, private?"

"Jerry, sir."

"Jerry. You can watch, but don't move."

Some guys liked to watch their flesh and bone get reknit. These were the same guys who liked to watch them get stitched up without anesthesia.

Brent held his right hand over the wound. The piece of the ulna moved back into place and the bone started to grow. Brent led the growth with his hand, joined it to the other broken bones near his wrist.

Then came the muscles and tendons. It was like drawing with energy, each line a part of the muscle, flowing from tendon to the muscle still there. It was slow going, because he wanted to do this right.

About half an hour later, he connected the arteries and veins, and, a short time after that, a sheen of pale white skin covered the wound.

Brent said, "You'll feel pain when I let go. Ready?"

Jerry nodded and Brent let go. Jerry let out a yelp. However, tears came unbidden to his eyes. Brent knew from experience about the pain of the blood flowing into new tissue.

"I would not throw bowling balls with that just yet," said Brent. "Doc, can he have light duty for a couple of weeks?"

"Aw, man," moaned Jerry.

"Better than a medical discharge," said the Army doctor. "I'll get the paperwork."

"But —"

"No," said Brent firmly. "You can practice on the range and go easy on it in the gym, okay?"

Jerry flexed his fingers. Brent knew he would be feeling pain as he did it.

"PT?" asked the doctor from beyond the curtain.

Brent looked at the Marine. Jerry certainly was one of those Marines who would have to be forced to take it easy. "Yes, physical therapy for his fingers, dexterity."

"Got it."

To Jerry, Brent asked, "Play an instrument? Piano? Guitar?"

"Guitar a few years back."

"Pick it up again. It'll help with the muscle development."

"Okay, thanks. I mean it. I didn't know you wizards could do shit like this."

"I'm a magus. It's what I do."

Brent heard someone come in. He turned to see Olron, looking around and wrinkling up his nose.

"Hey," said Olron, looking at the man's arm, surprised.

"Hey," Jerry said, putting his arm down. He looked warily at Olron.

Then both together said, "Look, I'm sorry —" "I'm sorry, man —"

They both laughed. Olron said, "He did a really nice job."

"Yeah. Fuckin' amazing shit."

The doctor came back into the room. "Here are your orders, private. They're already on their way to your CO. Tell your team leader what's up." The doctor stepped out. "And don't fuck up," he called from the other room.

"Yes, sir," said Jerry. He looked up at Olron. "Wanna play some video games?"

"Sure," said Olron.

Brent left, smiling.

At dusk, Brent found the container Shorty stayed in. Brent opened the door and heard the rambunctious yells of men on downtime. He saw some men gathered around an old TV, playing a video shooter game. Others were on laptops, had books, were bullshitting, playing cards, writing ...

"Can I help you, sir?" asked a bright red kid, sunburned on his cheeks, but not around his eyes due to the sunglasses. He had reverse raccoon eyes.

"I'm looking for Shorty."

"Oh, sure, I just saw him — hey, Boggs, you seen Shorty?"

Boggs, another bright red kid with a little fuzz for hair pointed vaguely to his left, at men gathered around a laptop.

"Fuck that!" yelled one of the men, slapping his thighs and sitting back, but his eyes still on the screen. "She can't fuckin' do that."

The other men roared. Brent went to the group. So intent on what they were watching, they didn't see him approach. All six of the men were wide-eyed and grinning. Brent thought he could hear a woman's breathless moans coming from the laptop.

"'scuse me," said Brent.

They all looked up. Some paled. Some blushed. One slammed shut the laptop.

"I'm looking for Shorty."

All of them turned to look at a short brick house of a man. All shoulders and chest, bald, with shining blue eyes and blushing, he looked down from their gaze. He glanced to his right, then stood up, meeting Brent's eyes and saluting.

"Yes, sir." Brent could see the stretching of the fabric across his groin.

"Can I speak with you a moment?"

Shorty swallowed, climbed over a cot. At his full height, he came up to Brent's eyes. Brent tilted his head toward the door.

"You're one of the dragon riders?" Brent asked.

"Yes, sir. I ride Makrah."

Brent held out his hand. "I'm Brent. I'm the new liaison."

Shorty shook the hand, a very tight grip. "The girls mentioned you, sir."

"I hope I wasn't interrupting anything in there."

"No, sir, just watching a movie." Shorty shoved his hands in his pockets.

Brent knew damn well what kind of movie. If the higher-ups caught them, they'd be punished because it was against Islamic law to have porn of any kind. And when in Afghanistan, they had to follow those customs.

"Well," said Brent, "I just wanted to introduce myself."

"What's going to happen to Waters?"

"I don't know. New assignment, I guess." However, if he won the battle later on, the man would be so severely injured that he would be sent home. Brent was betting on it.

Shorty nodded. He stood uncomfortably until Brent said, "See you later?"

"Yes, sir," Shorty said, offering the salute first and nearly running back into the barracks.

5

ASIDE

*H*i, Brent,

I hope you're doing okay. We miss you. Pickles is back to being his old mopey self now that you're gone.

Keithy went to court and got disability. At least now he'll have some money coming in. Most of it will be for rent, I suppose. He won't have any more of those big parties. He almost got arrested for having pot, but he has a doctor's note and they let it go, even though medical marijuana isn't legal here.

Your father found out that the man who kidnapped you "allegedly" committed suicide in his cell. This was before any trials. Your father doesn't think it was a suicide, but no one is investigating.

The Indian restaurant where they found you was owned by some Pakistanis. Your father can't investigate. As far as the police are concerned, the case is closed. We're lucky you were alive. I prayed for you every day. Luke was amazing.

By the way, Luke is going back to France at the end of the year. They put a req up to find a new detective. Your father might end up with Tony as a partner. He said if Larry is his partner, he's quitting.

Lori is finally looking into getting some help for Ashley. She heard from Keithy about disability so she wants to get it for her. Dante got kicked out of daycare again. He bit a little girl. They said he's dangerous. Lori's shopping around for another one, her third this year.

One of the NP's left the doctor's group and he's not bothering to look for a replacement. He said he has enough patients to keep him busy and as they leave he won't take any new ones. He's looking to retire in five years. I hope I can find something else at my age.

I'm glad you're not in Iraq. They're having a hard time there. That's what CNN says. I don't like to watch the news anymore. It makes me depressed.

Love you, miss you. Stay safe.
Love,
Mom
P.S. Share the cookies.

★   ★   ★

Dear Brent,

This is my first letter I'm writing to you. It's been three days since you left. I was busy working. I picked up more hours.

I don't know what you want me to talk about. Things are okay. I liked having you over. For a few reasons.

Keith didn't have the party on Friday. I don't know how long that will last. The cops must have found out. Things are very quiet now.

Keith isn't happy much anymore. He usually stands at the door if I come over. He doesn't invite me in anymore. I see an older woman come in with groceries for him now. Maybe he's got one of those CNA helpers.

I guess I'm supposed to say I miss you and all that jazz. I miss you.

Oh, my car! I didn't get to tell you. They told me I had to get a new alternator and a battery. They sell batteries at Wal-Mart for $50. They charged me $110 for a new battery!!! It was $500 for the alternator. A rebuilt one too!!! They said my car was old. It's only 5 years old. Can you burn their place down or something when you get back?!

I bought Disney stamps. I hope you like them. I'll save them just for you. I'll send you another letter when things get exciting.

Stay out of trouble!
Luv — Chrissie

6

KUNAR PROVINCE

B RENT GATHERED THE LETTERS into a small pile with an elastic band around them. His mother's letter had given him goosebumps. He wondered about the Pakistanis she wrote about; the Black Lions must be a militant group of Taliban or Pakistanis.

He lay back on the cot and put out the mage light to catch a few hours' sleep. When the alarm went off at 0130, he didn't bother putting up a light. He pulled on his uniform and grabbed the staff.

Stars filled the black sky, but their light was eclipsed by the half-moon hanging low in the horizon. Brent yawned and headed out to the latrine. He saw some groups of men milling about near the helicopters, getting ready for their night patrols.

Brent stood near the latrine after finishing his business. He thought about standing up the guy, but he knew that wouldn't fly in magic circles. Mage duels, good-natured sparring, was encouraged. It made the magus stronger, they said. It actually created bad blood between people.

He got to the dragons' tent, the farthest point north of the airfield.

Waters appeared seemingly out of nowhere. "Rogers."

Brent jumped. "Lieutenant," he said coldly.

Waters looked around. "We might as well do it here."

"I guess."

"C'mon. You were so gung-ho about it before."

Brent said nothing. thinking of the duels during training, how he almost lost his hair and eyebrows to a Torch, a fire magus.

Waters grinned. "Just think: After this, you'll never see me again."

"All right, let's get this over with."

They walked past the dragon's tent. Baldar stepped out, saw them walking past, and ducked back into the tent.

The two men went to an empty area of the airfield, but well-lit by natural light. Brent and Waters stood back to back.

"Fifty paces," said Waters.

Brent thought that was going to be too close, but, before he could protest, Waters started counting off his paces. Brent jumped and walked the fifty steps, whirled, and slammed his staff into the ground, putting up the shield.

Waters' fireball exploded against the shield. Brent didn't feel any heat, so it was just a flashy fireball, not made with real fire.

Waters kept battering him with fireballs, starting off yellow and red, then turning white. Brent knew if he got hit by one of those phosphorous flames, he'd be burned.

When Waters paused for a second, a spell in Brent's mind let go at the same instant he slammed his staff top-down into the ground. The fire got past his shield and caught on his leg. While he fell to put it out, the ground beneath him rumbled.

Brent's spell broke as a geyser of earth burst upward from the sand, right in front of Waters. Rocks, dirt, and sand rained down on Waters. He had a shield up, so nothing hit him.

Brent rose. His leg throbbed. He did not make any motion, just thought the spell, an easy spell, one he used nearly every day.

Waters flew up into the air, his arms and legs flailing. His shield formed a green ball around him. Brent raised his hands, lifting Waters higher up in the air. Then Brent thrust his hands downward. Waters plummeted to the ground from about thirty meters in the air.

Brent heard a woman cheer but ignored it as he dashed over to Waters. He moved around the hole he had made, to see Waters getting up, brushing himself off.

Waters whirled, throwing something. Brent flinched, closing his eyes before setting up a shield. Something hit his chest.

He looked down to see a group of small daggers, about a dozen of them, embedded in his skin. He pulled out the one from his chest and felt the rest grow an inch or so larger.

"Good luck, First Magus," said Waters, laughing and walking away.

Brent looked down at the remainder of the daggers. He pulled one out closest to his heart. The others grew longer and wider.

He turned around. The female riders came running over to him, the dragons gathered at the front of their tent.

Jen said, "What the fuck?"

"When you take one out, the others grow larger," said Brent, pulling one from his stomach. He winced. Blood seeped from the wound. He had never seen this spell before.

"He was trying to kill you!"

Brent nodded. If he survived this, he was going to hurt Waters. At least.

Meghan said, "This one in your shoulder, we can leave it for last."

"Unless they grow as big as swords," said Debbie.

Brent didn't like that idea.

"What if you take them all out at once?"

"I don't know," Brent said. "But let's try it."

The dragons backed away as each of the women took two blades. Brent asked, "Ready?"

They all nodded or said, "Yep."

"Three. Two. One." Brent held his breath.

All of them pulled the daggers out at the same time, and blood oozed out from the wounds. Brent put a hand on his stomach to try and heal the wound, but it wouldn't stop. The daggers were bloody, but the same size as they had been in his body. They dropped the daggers in the dirt.

Brent said, weaving back and forth, his vision getting cloudy, "I think I need a medic."

"I'll get one," said Meghan. Carrying one of the daggers with her, she rushed to the red cross container.

"At least you're not gushing blood, said Debbie.

"Can someone collect those daggers?" Brent fell against Debbie. Jen picked them up.

The medic, a Marine, showed up with Meghan.

"What's this about a stab wound?" the medic said.

Jen held up the daggers.

"Can you walk?" asked the medic.

"Yeah," said Brent.

"Somebody come with us to the hospital."

Jen shoved the daggers into her belt. She and Debbie flanked Brent as they walked the short distance to the first aid container.

"Who did this, Sergeant?" demanded the medic.

Brent looked away. "Don't worry. I'll take care of it."

The women glanced at each other. There was a saying, "Don't piss off a mage." With Brent's angry countenance, they didn't want any spells to come in their direction.

At medops, the doctor pointed to a gurney for Brent to sit. Olron appeared, looking concerned.

Brent forced a smile. "Don't worry. It's only magic."

"I know," said Olron. "This doesn't mean a mage war, does it?"

"A mage war?"

"Dragons were used in mage wars."

When? Brent wondered.

The doctor commanded, "Get your clothes off."

Brent shrugged out of his bloody shirt and the t-shirt underneath.

"Can't you heal these?" asked the doctor, putting on a pair of gloves.

"Magic can't stop magic. It's like fire on fire."

He examined the wounds on his chest and leg. "If I were you, I wouldn't 'take care of' anything for a while."

"He did try to kill me."

"Then I'll report it to his superior, and we'll get the little shit discharged. Just because you're in the Magicorps doesn't mean that you're above the law of the Armed Forces. Besides, they outlawed dueling in the early 1800's."

Brent watched as he worked. The riders had disappeared, and Olron left soon after, a concerned look on his face.

The doctor washed his hands when he finished, saying, "No heavy lifting for three days."

Brent grunted and jumped off the table. "Thanks."

"Welcome. No more duels."

"Not here."

The doctor sighed and went to his computer. Brent went bare-chested out to his cot.

When he got there, he took out an almost-clean shirt. He gathered up his kit. *No heavy lifting. Right.*

His little duel didn't stop the dragon patrols. He heard in the TOC that Makrah was going to be followed by the visiting Marine Wing commander, Captain Joseph Laurence. Brent was able to hitch a ride with Captain Laurence and Lieutenant Waters, who looked smug and acted like nothing happened that morning. Brent glared at him as they rode in the noisy Humvee.

"So what can they do?" asked Captain Laurence.

Waters took the question before Brent could reply. "They can fly at high altitudes. They see what goes on below. If we flush out Taliban, they can chase them down."

"That's all you use them for?"

"We were thinking of using them for recon, but they don't have any radios."

"Why not?"

"The riders have parachutes."

"They don't need parachutes. Give 'em all radios."

Waters, without a blink, said "Yes, sir."

Brent opened his mouth, then snapped it shut. How much could he get away with being part of the Magic Corps and outranked?

"Once we give them radios, they can recon. Are they bullet-proof?"

"Yes, sir."

Brent stared at Waters. He knew from today that they were afraid of magic. That meant something made them mortal.

"Then have them fly closer. Have them fly sand into those bastard's beards."

"Sir, they don't speak our language in dragon form, at least not that I know."

"For Christ's sake, Waters, give the fucking soldiers the radios and have *them* do the reporting."

Brent had to butt in. "I don't think the riders are bullet-proof." When the captain looked sharply at Brent, he hastily added, "Sir."

"I don't believe I asked you, Master Sergeant Rogers."

Waters grinned. *You prick*, Brent thought.

"Sorry, sir. I'm a healing wizard, but I can't bring someone back from the dead."

"You don't know Marines, Rogers. We're tougher than you think."

"Understood, sir," said Brent quietly.

Laurence thought out loud: "They can also be used as a show of force, since they're bullet-proof. They can fly in close and terrorize."

Brent said, "Sir, we're trying not to send villagers into a panic."

"Says who?"

"They were orders from upper command."

From the start of his deployment, they were meant to be assistants to the Afghan National Army and Afghan National Police. The ANA and ANP were supposed to do the heavy lifting.

"Well, I'm CO and I'm telling you I don't give two fucking shits about any of these backward fucking villages. We need to assume they're all helping the Taliban. This close to the Paki border, they have to be."

"But, sir, the elections."

"What about them?"

"We need people to come out, sir. If we act like oppressors, they won't come out."

"You one of those liberal hippies, son? You believe we're out to bring democracy to these fucking heathens?"

"Sir, our orders from Lieutenant General Hillier said that our primary mission is to get people out for the election."

"Then he's a fuckin' hippie. We're fighting a *War On Terror*, son. People are dying for a democracy. I'm making sure it stops here and now. By the way, what the fuck are you doing here, Wizard?"

"My orders are to be a liaison between command and the dragons."

"What are you doing *here*. In this fucking Humvee?"

"I need to find out what they can do. Their needs."

"They're soldiers. They don't have *needs*."

"Sir, if you don't give them what they need, you'll have a smoking ruin of a base."

"How the fuck do you know?"

"I'm a magus, sir."

"So?"

"I know magic."

"These fucking dragons, they're magic?"

"Yes, sir."

Laurence looked from Waters to Brent. Waters looked steadily at Laurence.

"Bullshit.," said Laurence. "You can tell them that. They use our tents, eat our food, work with our men. We treat them like the soldiers they are."

"Like the ANA?"

"Yeah." Laurence paused, rubbing his chin. "Yeah, like the ANA."

That wasn't going to be good. Some in the Army treated the ANA like crap, and he assumed this Marine commander thought the same thing.

The radio crackled and Brent paid attention, "Frostfire on target." Brent translated again: *Makrah is at the village.*

"Stop," said Laurence.

After the driver did, Laurence got out. He took out his binoculars, turning east.

Brent and Waters got out also, staying close to the vehicle in case of a mine.

Laurence is a boss or an idiot, Brent thought.

Brent saw a dot in the sky that he assumed was a dragon or a plane.

Laurence said, "That thing's fuckin' smart. It put a wall of ice around the village. I gotta see this."

They all piled back into the vehicle and headed to the village. Brent couldn't look at Waters without thinking about how to hurt him and make it look like an accident.

Marine Compass company, "The Pathfinders," was already there. The captain in charge greeted Laurence.

"We think we have our objective in there, sir."

He pointed to the ice wall around the western end of the village. The south was a wilted orchard, where Makrah sat, his rider resting in the saddle. Brent left Waters and Laurence behind as he approached Makrah.

Makrah raised his head when Brent came into view. He let out a rumble and bared his teeth.

"Hey, Shorty!" Brent called up to the rider.

"Yes, sir," he said, with a wide grin on his face.

Brent heard the booming voice of the captain, yelling up at Makrah. If dragons could look full of contempt, Makrah did. He gazed down at the small group of men was if they were gnats.

"You the rider?" demanded Laurence.

"Yes, sir," said Shorty.

"Give over your parachute."

With no complaint, Shorty slipped down and took off the pack and handed it over. A man stepped up and helped Shorty into the radio pack. It was much heavier than the 'chute.

"There," said Laurence, as they fit a headset on him. "You're live now."

Said Waters, "You'll be getting direct orders from now on instead of having to land to receive orders."

Brent watched Shorty nod. The Marines weren't thinking. They couldn't be constantly flying. They, either the riders or the dragons, needed rest every once in a while.

What if a heat-seeking missile came at them? What would happen to the riders, then? The dragons could probably outmaneuver it, but the riders would plummet like a rock.

Shorty tried out the radio. "Understood," he said. "Affirmative."

He went to the dragon. Makrah lay flat, and Shorty was able to use a rope that hung off the left side of the dragon's neck attached to the saddle. He leaned forward on the saddle and spoke to Makrah.

Makrah launched into the air from a sitting position like a helo taking off, sending up dirt and dust everywhere on top of the men gathered there.

Brent turned away to avoid getting dirt in his eyes and mouth.

"That bastard did that intentionally," muttered Waters.

After spitting out dirt, Laurence said, "Let's find the other dragons. You all keep doing what you're doing. Wizard!"

"Yes, sir," Brent started to follow.

"You stay here with the Pathfinders."

"Yes, sir." He tried not to sound petulant, but he felt it.

He looked at the lieutenant of the company, who gave him a tiny shrug. Captain Laurence marched back to his Humvee. Waters gave Brent a grin. Brent tapped the ground with his staff. The ground raised up — Waters tripped and almost went sprawling. Brent turned away, following the company's lieutenant.

Something nagged at him about Waters and the dragons. Something ... wrong.

When Brent dismounted back at Blessing, Olron waited for him, wearing a pair of shorts and nothing else.

"What's this about new orders?" he demanded of Brent.

Brent headed to the latrine. "Fifth Wing's CO says he wants to use you more in the fight."

"What's next, strapping bombs to our bellies?"

"Shh. Don't say that too loud. They might get ideas."

He entered the latrine and Olron followed.

"We're not planes. We can be injured, even killed. We're not fast like your planes. We're agile, but not when we have riders. We're not armored. We can't keep your riders safe."

"I tried to explain that, but the new commander has different ideas. You can thank Waters for that." He finished taking a leak, then glared at Olron. "Do you mind?"

"I thought you were our liaison?" Olron didn't move.

"It seems to me that Lieutenant Waters knows a lot more about you than I do. He's not forthcoming with information, though. I'm going to talk to him in private," Brent said, leaving the latrine.

"Like you did this morning?"

"I can be professional when I have to." He refrained from scratching at the stitches.

"I'll go with you," said Olron, following.

Obviously, Olron didn't understand "private", but Brent was too tired and too frustrated to argue with him. He wanted to save his energy for the real argument to come.

Brent first started with HQ, but Waters wasn't there. He wasn't at TOC, either. Brent asked around, to learn where the container the lieutenant stayed in.

As he walked toward it, he saw four MP's flanking Waters as they crossed the compound. Brent stopped. Olron bumped into Brent.

"Oh, no. They didn't," said Brent, watching the men walk past them.

Waters didn't see Brent.

"Who didn't what?"

"Someone called on him about the duel. Probably the doctor."

"What now?"

Brent said nothing, watching Waters stiffly walk between the men, heading to the brig.

Olron said, changing the subject, "We need food. What are you going to do about that?"

"I don't know," Brent said quietly. "I really don't know."

"Then we will go hunting." Olron grinned with those wicked teeth. "You wouldn't be happy with what we hunt, however."

Brent had to find food — and fast.

7

FOB BLESSING

W HEN BRENT BEGGED THE MESS COOK for some meat, he was told, "I don't feed fuckin' stray animals."

Brent wasn't sure what that meant, but he was able to get a side of frozen beef anyway.

The dragons fell on the meat like starving men, tearing into it and crunching bones. Makrah came away with a full leg, Tyrath with a haunch, Baldar and Olron sharing the rest. Brent couldn't watch.

Makrah said, leaning back, "This is a good snack."

Brent told him, "Sorry, but that's your dinner."

All four of the dragons froze.

"This?" growled Tyrath.

"Look," Brent snarled, "if you don't like it, go fight on the other fucking side."

He stormed back to his container and walked down to his room at the end. *To hell with this*, he thought.

This time, the room was full of Marines. "Oh, hey," one of them said, pointing to Brent's cot. "That your shit?"

"Yeah," said Brent flatly.

The Marine nodded. Brent knew sleeping alone in weak air conditioning would be too good to last.

He thought he was tired enough, but he couldn't sleep with the men there. His mind raced with how he was going to control and feed the dragons.

Finally, Brent slipped on his night vision goggles and left the room. He stepped out of the climate-controlled container into the cool summer air.

The NVG's used the moonlight to coat everything green. He walked toward the latrine. He heard a footfall on gravel. He stopped, his blood pumping hard in his ears. He had forgotten his staff at the cot.

He scanned the area with his goggles but saw nothing. He heard the noise again — footfalls nearby.

Brent extended his senses, but when he did, something came at him from behind. A man's arms wrapped around him, one around his head, pulling the goggles down over his mouth, and the other arm around his torso. He held Brent like a lover, pressing his body into Brent's back.

"We've been watching you, Sorcerer." The man spoke in Pakistani-accented English. "You know us."

Brent summoned up some magic, the spell in mind, to push the man off him. He let loose, but nothing happened.

He grunted as he got slammed in the gut as the magic bounced back onto him.

The man chuckled. "You sorcerers never learn."

Brent resorted to his military training. He tried to tuck his hand between their bodies to grab the guy's nuts. The man held him in a vise grip.

"We took you before. We can take you again."

Brent moved his feet in the sand to try and hook around the other man's foot, but the other man was rooted to the spot. He tried to push back or lean forward, but he couldn't move.

The man chuckled into Brent's neck. "We will destroy you, Sorcerer. You and your beasts."

The man shoved his body against Brent. He fell forward, his hands out to catch himself from slamming face-first into the ground. Brent shoved the NVG's up to his eyes. As he expected, the man was gone.

When got back to his container, he saw some men getting ready for a night patrol.

"Fuckin' seek 'n' peek," whispered one of the men as Brent walked by. The Marines gathered their kits and filed out, leaving him in relative silence.

He got back in bed and lay awake, wondering about who had jumped him: *How did he get in?* Were all the Black Lions immune to magic? Brent got up, knowing sleep had escaped him now.

Hi mom

Things are really busy here. They changed my orders so that now I'm in charge of a small group of [he paused as he struggled for the best way to put it] rangers and recon soldiers. They're a special group with their own designation. I can't tell you much about them because it's classified.

So far, it's been interesting. No severe firefights [he lied], just potshots. The worst is trying to find supplies for the troops, because of all the bureaucratic red tape. I fill out a form in triplicate and by the time I get approval my guys are counting bullets.

Tell dad that I'm probably not going to go on the dole unless —God forbid—I get injured. I've been lucky so far. Knock on wood for me.

He wanted to put something in about the Black Lions, but that would worry his mother. He sat back and looked around the room, lit only by his image light. He always had a hard time with these letters home.

Finally, he concluded:

A lot of stuff happened but I can't discuss it. Classified. Just know that I'm safe. I'm keeping everyone safe, too.

Thanks for the cookies. Send more.
Love, Brent

He sealed the envelope, then got a paper for Chrissie.

Hey, Chrissie,

I know that working at Wal-Mart is the most exciting job next to mine. I hope it's not too exciting because I know how exciting things get here.

Things are going okay. We were involved in a firefight a couple of days ago. One of my team was killed because I wasn't there. They gave me new orders, so now I'm with a Marine ranger/recon group. Marines don't have magi, so I'm allowed to go across the armed forces. I've been mostly with the Army which is why I have the Army rank of Master Sergeant.

My new platoon includes women. They're in a combat role which is unusual even for Marines. At least I think it's combat. Any time you're getting shot at is combat, in my opinion. They're just as good as the men, I think.

I'm a liaison between them, mostly administrative, but some combat. I don't like the administrative shit because it's boring. I didn't sign up for that. I like mixing it up, getting out there and fighting. They say it's the adrenaline rush and that's probably true. But it's what I enjoy, what I like. I miss it. Don't tell my mom!

The Marines are badass, like you'd think they were. They think nothing of going into the battle. They're all tough motherfuckers and I have a lot of respect for them.

I got into a fight with another magus. I got hurt, but not bad, maybe 70 stitches. I'll show you the scars when I come home again.

That won't be for at least a year. The way the Army works is most times a year's break, and you're home for a month. I skipped my first year's break because I thought I was needed. I signed up for five years' total—what was I thinking, right? But I enjoy this.

I don't know what they're going to do after the election here in October, if we're still going to be here or going to Iraq. I heard Iraq is tough with the mujahideen. They can be just as bad here.

I guess that's all I have that I can share. The weather is hot. I've gotten sunburned a few times already. We're all waiting around for October.

Don't let the excitement at Wal-Mart get to you.

He paused as he thought how to sign it. Finally, he compromised.

See you soon — Brent

That morning, in the pre-dawn hours, Brent left his container and saw a figure in the dark standing at the dragons' tent. Brent started to approach, noting he was bald.

The man turned to him. "Wizard," Baldar said.

Brent gave him a nod.

He looked up at the sky for a moment. "See the sky? It looks like home."

"Where's home?"

"Antarctica."

"Are there a lot of dragons in Antarctica?"

"Not anymore."

"Why?" Brent got closer. He felt chilly next to him.

"We are old. Dying." He focused on Brent. "Are you here to use us?"

"What?"

"That is what a wizard is for, to use us." He stared, unblinking at Brent. "You have given us new orders to fly low, and we must obey."

"Or what?"

"You will destroy us."

Brent laughed. Baldar stepped back.

Brent said, "Why would I do that?"

"That is not why you are here? To make sure we do your bidding?"

"No, that's up to the military." Brent closed the distance. "Look, Baldar, I don't like the new orders any more than you do. I'm going to try and get them rescinded somehow."

Although, he thought, *the brass won't like it.*

He remembered Archmage Dieter's words, "Remember who you work for."

Baldar face showed no emotion. "I do not trust you, Wizard. Words. You are full of words, not action. Where is our food? We will hunt tomorrow evening if you do not bring us food."

"Hunt what?"

"What do you think? People."

Baldar went back into the tent, leaving Brent to mull that over in the chill morning air.

If food was what they wanted, food he'd have to get. Brent stood like a beggar outside the rear of the mess tent when the first KP men showed up.

The chef in charge that morning wasn't the head chef. No, he didn't know where they could get fresh meat. In fact, they didn't get their own meat fresh, but had it shipped from home because they couldn't trust the local people to not poison them.

Brent needed orders from his CO, the Archmage, to order them to give him fresh meat from the kitchen. He didn't have time to go to Camp Phoenix in Kabul, plead his case, and return. He would have to go above Waters since he was now in the pokey. That meant at least a captain.

The door to HQ was open and lights on inside the rough-hewn wooden area. Smelling of fresh wood, desks consisting of sawhorses with planks across them, or plastic white folding tables with uncomfortable-looking folding chairs set behind them formed a line like school desks.

"Hello?" Brent called.

"Yes, sir." Someone popped up from under a desk.

"I'm looking for Lieutenant Waters' superior."

"That would be Major Keagan, sir. He's not in yet."

Brent pointed to a curtained-off area. "His office over there?"

The young private pointed in front of Brent. "Two desks down, sir."

Right near the door. There were no chairs in front of his desk, and the desk looked empty. "I'll wait for him."

"Yes, sir." Brent wove his way through to the desk near the major's and sat down.

The private disappeared under the desk again.

"Do you know where Lieutenant Waters' desk is, private?"

"I'm rewriting it now, sir."

Brent turned in his chair. "Did he leave behind any files?"

"No, sir."

Damn, Brent thought. *He did this intentionally; I know he did. Left me to flounder.*

"You wouldn't happen to know where he got food for the dragons, do you?"

"Sorry, sir. I didn't work with him." He poked his head up from under the desk again. "Maybe the base's depot?"

Brent rose, an internal light bulb of realization going off. "Good idea."

At daybreak, Brent traversed the base westward. He ended up in front of a container with a warehouse, containing everything the modern army required. Even this early, there were men in t-shirts lugging boxes of ammo and weapons, clothing and mail, food and medicine. He threaded his way through a container to an air-conditioned office in the back.

He knocked on the door, not really expecting an answer this early.

"Come in," said a man's voice.

Brent stepped inside. He saluted the man behind the desk, assuming he was at least a lieutenant or above. The man behind the desk gave him the stern look of a typical Marine officer who brokered no bullshit.

"Can I help you?" he said after returning Brent's salute.

"Sir. I'm looking for provisions for the Fifth Wing."

"The Fifth Wing? You mean the dragons?"

"Yes, sir," he said.

"Where's Lieutenant Waters?"

"Reassigned, sir. I'm working with them now."

"You're not a Marine."

"No, sir. Army. I'm a magus."

"I see."

Brent continued, "Sir, basically, I need meat for the dragons."

"I'm afraid it's spoken for here." The second lieutenant leaned forward, putting his head on a steeple of his fingers. "What if you went to the locals, bought your meat there?"

Brent didn't want to deal with the locals. They may have worked for the Taliban and might poison the meat to make the dragons sick. He didn't know if he should take that kind of a risk.

"Do you think that's safe?"

"What're they going to do, strap a bomb to a goat?"

If he didn't get food for the dragons today, they would forage, and it wouldn't be pretty. They would kill innocents and Taliban alike.

"Take some men to Gimblr, right nearby. We have a good relationship with the locals. Do you have American money? They'll take that."

"Yes, sir, I have some money."

He leaned back. "Buy some goats, or cows, or whatever they have. Otherwise, the dragons will turn on us, won't they?"

"In short, yes, sir."

"We have a special fund for things like this. Talk to one of the battalion commanders, and we'll get this straightened out."

Brent felt a huge weight off his shoulders. "Yes, sir. Thank you, sir."

"Take a truck and four men. Tell them Lieutenant Tai said so if they give you any grief."

Gimblr was about 20 minutes by truck from FOB Blessing. After going back to his container to get the translation stone and his staff, Brent commandeered two battered Ford Ranger trucks and four burly men with guns.

Brent got into one of the four-by-four trucks and noticed that it was a stick shift, which he hadn't driven since Boot camp, and only once. He checked to make sure that the gas was full. He looked at one of the other men and then glanced meaningfully at the shifter. The man smiled and took the driver's seat. Brent sat in the middle, between two big Marines. The other two took the other truck.

They drove for a little while down the makeshift military road. As he got to the end which turned into a T, he realized he had forgotten a map. But the Marines knew where they were going and took a right-hand turn onto the highway.

They passed assorted men with their beasts of burden walking on the side of the road. The road was hardened dirt, not even asphalt. It ended up in a village surrounded by houses, some two or three stories high. They drove slowly down the main street, avoiding children, chickens, and women in burqas.

They drove to the well in the center of town. The men dismounted from the two trucks, hands near the triggers of their guns, warily looking out at the people. Women gathered their items and disappeared.

"What do we do, sarge?" asked one of the men to Brent.

"They'll show up out of curiosity," Brent said, just as a group of men stepped out of a building.

The group paused, but two men came up to them from the group. The rest of the men — elders, Brent assumed — remained behind glaring at the troops, who gave it right back.

Of the two men, one spoke in perfect English. "What do you want?" He also looked more westernized, in a t-shirt and long, loose pants.

Brent held the stone loosely in his hand, but it seemed like he didn't need it. "I'm looking for some goats."

The men looked at each other. The one who didn't speak muttered, "What do they want goats for?"

Brent interrupted, "I'm sure that you have seen our dragons."

The two men stopped talking to each other and whipped their heads to Brent, shock and recognition apparent on their faces.

"If we do not feed them, they will hunt. Probably here first."

The English-speaker glanced back at the group of men.

He turned back to Brent and said, "One moment."

He put his arm around his companion's shoulders and dragged him back to the elders.

Brent couldn't hear what they said, but their voices were loud, arguing. The four Marines had their eyes everywhere at once, while Brent only watched the elders. One man peeled off from the group, stomping angrily away. The English-speaker returned alone.

"Ahmad will return with goats."

"I will pay him, of course."

He stiffened in surprise momentarily, then he nodded. "Of course."

Ahmad and a skinny boy returned with four goats, their bellies distended, their legs like sticks. Brent peeled off twenty dollars of his own money and handed it to Ahmad, who readily took it.

Brent said, "I need four goats every afternoon. I will pay twenty dollars for them. Tell that to the elders, would you?"

"Yes," said the English speaker.

"I'll be back tomorrow."

"I will tell the elders."

Brent turned to the Marines. "Let's load them up."

They each easily lifted the goats into the two trucks.

Brent had the Marines drive up to the airstrip. They stopped outside the dragons' tent, looking for extra stakes to tie the goats to. Brent ended up having them tie the goats up to the stakes of the tent instead. As they did, he saw one of the dragons come in for a landing.

It was Baldar, the sun glinting off his armor. The dragon landed about two hundred meters away from them. Debbie dismounted, and they stripped him of his saddle. Brent and the men waited with the nervous goats.

"Holy shit, he's fuckin' huge," said one of the men.

"He's blue," said another.

"He's a frost dragon," said Brent.

Baldar, in dragon form, flew over to the tent. Baldar looked down at the goats. The goats gathered together, bleating in terror. The men bunched up as well, though not in terror, still wary at the size of the dragon and how small they were compared to it.

Baldar tilted his head at Brent who motioned to the goats. "Take one."

Baldar ducked down, snatched one of the goats by its neck and yanked it up. The rope stopped him from pulling the goat away entirely. One of the Marines ran over and cut the rope with a knife while the goat screamed. Baldar took a hold of the goat and tore out its throat, covering his chest armor with splatters of blood.

Brent turned to watch the men, who winced as Brent could hear the crunch of bone and the last bleat of the dying animal. But they watched. Brent turned to see the dragon tear through the goat's innards and split the goat in half. His stomach flipped. The remaining goats screamed but couldn't run away.

He didn't want to be around for the rest of the dragons to have their feast. "Okay, guys, show's over. Let's go."

The men mounted up and drove back to the depot muttering awestruck, "Fuuuuuck, man."

8

KUNAR PROVINCE

BRENT KNEW IT WAS THE WEEK of the full moon because of the howling.

Days before, during, and after the full moon, werewolves came out. Some men, knowing that their inner beasts were wild, locked themselves up so they wouldn't hunt. Some others attached themselves to the K9 units for the three days of their change.

Their handlers were soldiers picked from the ranks and didn't have to go through the intense training that K9 handlers did. Werewolves could also shift at will, if necessary. Some chose to remain with the K9's; some became handlers, alphas to their dogs.

Then there were the soldiers that could shift in middle of battle and become the half-man, half-berserker beast of movies and legend. They were not allowed to shift unless their life, or the lives of their comrades, were in imminent danger. Too often, Brent heard stories of soldiers discharged because they shifted into the wolf-man at the wrong time.

Early in the morning, Brent got up in the dark, empty container. He hadn't heard the platoon of Marines leave. *Obviously more tired than I thought*, he reckoned, as he got dressed in the dark.

Brent stood in the chill morning air, watching the riders with their radios. The dragons were ready for flight. What if the dragons had their own radios? They could listen. They didn't have to talk. They would be called in as needed.

As he wondered about that, he went to the TOC and found Makrah's route. He went back to his cot, shrugged into his full kit, and, with his staff, he headed out to the HLZ. A small group of wolves and their handlers split up among the transport helos, joining different platoons.

Brent had to ask around before he found one of the helos going to a place within Makrah's perimeter. He boarded the bird along with two wolves. They didn't have to be in crates, like normal dogs, though they still wore harnesses and leashes.

Brent sat across from one team. Larger than the usual German Shepherd, the wolf easily fit in the seat. He looked at Brent and winked.

"What's his name?" Brent asked the man seated next to the wolf.

"Kurt," he said. "He's a mechanic."

Brent remembered the big man who came up to him on his first day meeting the dragons. "What's your name?"

"Billy," said the man. Billy's body shape was unknown under the kit, but he was about Brent's height. "You going to overwatch?"

"I'm supposed to watch for dragons."

"Ever see them at work?"

"Just one."

"I haven't."

"They're a sight to see. I saw the ice dragon."

"The big red dragon," said the other K9 handler, "he's fuckin' insane."

They both paid attention to him. "You've seen him?" asked Billy.

The man nodded. Then the helo's engines started, and all conversation stopped because of the noise.

Half an hour after dropoff, the helo took off into the night sky, leaving Brent, Billy, and his platoon in the middle of a desert. Wearing his night vision glasses like everyone else, Brent followed the men to their vantage point atop a hill, overlooking a serene village. The men waited for the wolves to sniff out mines, and then dug in.

After digging a small indentation for himself, Brent lay down and took off his goggles to look up at the sky, well-lit by the cloudless moon. Its brightness blotted out the lighter stars, but he could still see the brighter constellations.

He smiled as he picked out Orion and the Dippers. Orion was up late, and they themselves were late in the fighting season. The Marines could fight any time, any place, and prided themselves on it. Brent was proud to be serving with them—as he was with all the armed services that he had dealt with.

He then saw something cross the light of the stars. He put the goggles back on and tracked the motion. It was Makrah, swimming across the sky, crossing for a moment in front of the moon. As Makrah came closer, Brent saw his snake-like body moving like a wave, his head straight but his body constantly rising and falling.

"He's swimming," Brent said to no one in particular.

Makrah flew a circle around them, then flew directly up and north.

Hours passed. The sun rose. No one moved in the village. Brent wished he could somehow follow Makrah, to see where he was going. According to the perimeter map he memorized, the northern section was the southern part of Nuristan Province. Brent was at an empty village south of Nangalaam.

"Finally," someone said.

Brent looked behind them, away from the village, to see a truck coming their way. The truck stopped a few yards away, and deposited men of the Afghan National Army. They walked over to the other platoon, about sixty meters away from them. They were standing up, not bothering to try and hide. The Marines stayed down.

That's when the potshots from the village rang out. The ANA dove to the dirt and the men of Brent's platoon offered covering fire. Billy shot off his rifle while Kurt lay in the dirt, ready to jump up at a call from his handler.

Brent's magic didn't have the same range as the rifles. In a firefight like this, he was relatively worthless, unless they wanted him to send a flashy fireball in the village's general direction. It probably wouldn't catch on anything at this distance; besides, he wasn't a fire mage. He instead got out of the way of the soldiers doing their job.

Then an RPG blew up, just short of the platoon's position. At the same time, Brent heard a high-pitched roar.

Kurt barked, and Makrah wove his way toward them. Another RPG exploded, close enough to rain dust and dirt on them.

"Frostfire's on it," said the sergeant.

Brent watched the dragon swoop down, breathing bright blue fire at the village. Like Tyrath's fire, it caught on everything: burning and melting buildings, and probably the people inside them. A cheer went up. Makrah, his job done, flew off.

After what seemed like minutes but were probably mere seconds, one of the ANA got up. Someone from the village fired at him. He dropped.

"Oh, what the fuck —" muttered one man.

"A sniper," said a corporal, his mouth in the dirt while he peered out at the village from behind his semi-automatic weapon.

Brent glanced at Kurt and motioned upward with his hand. "We got this," said Brent, then looked at Billy. "If that's okay with you."

Billy undid the leash. "You guys go ahead. I'll cover you."

Brent and Kurt climbed out of the tiny foxhole and took a wide swing toward the village. Kurt and Brent searched for mines, avoiding one near the entrance to the village.

Buildings burned blue fire, smelling like melted steel. On the other side of the burning buildings stood a man before a courtyard wall with a hole small enough to aim a gun muzzle through.

Kurt and Brent watched as the man peered through a scope that was attached to the rifle, then placed the muzzle in the hole, feeding it beyond the wall. He looked ready to take another shot.

Kurt dashed across the few meters separating them from the man, tackling him. The gun fell out of the hole, clattering to the ground as the man fell face-first into the wall. Kurt bit into the man's shoulder and yanked him back hard, throwing him to the ground.

Brent ran to the man, thrusting the glowing end of the staff at his face. The man was just out of boyhood, not even with a beard. He raised his hands, while Kurt stood ready at Brent's right.

"Get up," said Brent, knowing the man couldn't understand him. He motioned upward with the staff.

The young man got up, eyes wide. Brent motioned again with the staff toward the village entrance. The young man started walking—limping, actually.

The shooting beyond the courtyard had stopped. Brent and Kurt herded the young man to the entrance of the village. Brent glanced at the buildings, now cracked and collapsed stone ruins.

Brent forced him to go faster. "Move," he said, thrusting the tip of the staff at the young man.

He seemed hesitant to walk. Kurt walked ahead of them, his nose to the street, sniffing for bombs.

They were met at the village entrance by some of the platoon Brent had arrived with. One of them dug up the mine that Brent and Kurt had avoided. They all waved or acknowledged Brent. Billy called Kurt over, while Brent turned the sniper over to the platoon sergeant.

Olron smelled of weed when Brent approached the dragons' tent. He was sitting outside and stood when Brent came into view.

"Makrah smoking again?" Brent asked.

"I think he's addicted." Olron motioned to the carpet for Brent to take a seat.

"Actually, I was looking for Baldar."

"Oh? What for?"

"I suspect he's got a thing about wizards."

"He does. It took months before he would even speak to Waters."

Brent scratched at the stitches on his shoulder. He had been doing so well, ignoring them. Now they all itched.

"I know where he is."

"Where?"

"With Shorty."

"I know where that is."

"Let me come with you." Olron placed a hand on Brent's arm, letting it linger.

Brent looked at the hand, then at Olron, who only smiled.

"Sure," said Brent, and pulled away.

They both walked side by side to the container with Shorty's company.

Olron nodded to the men outside, as if he was familiar with them, and held the door open for Brent. The place was loud, crowded as it had been before. Three TVs blared at once: two on two separate football games, and one on a video game. No one noticed Brent come in with the half-naked barefoot young man.

At the video game sat a bald man, roughly defined as male with broad shoulders and a flat chest.

"Baldar," called Olron over the uproar.

Baldar turned. He said something in that sweet language he used before with Makrah.

"I've brought the magus," said Olron.

Baldar's slitted white eyes focused on Brent. "It will have to wait. It is my turn when someone loses."

"I can wait," said Brent, looking at the TV. He couldn't see much in the dark of what looked like a cargo hold. Hell, he couldn't tell what the shooter was shooting at.

At the next scene, a man in armor was lying flat on a metal deck.

"Shit!" the player yelled, tossing his controller on a cot.

"Baldar!" called a man standing near the TV.

Baldar rose to his full height, a little taller than Brent. He pushed the chair aside and picked up the controller.

The other player walked over to Olron. "Wanna try?"

"No. I fight real battles."

"You?" He turned to Brent.

Brent shook his head. "I can't figure those things out."

Baldar started shooting at glowing blue targets that turned into puddles of blue goo on the metal decks of what seemed to be a spaceship. A group of men were all swarming along the decks. Baldar had joined them. One guy got up and filled the screen just as Baldar took aim.

"Get outta the way!" Baldar and some of the men yelled in unison.

Baldar moved around him and got hit. He dove behind a box.

The one who had stood up before got hit and also dove behind a crate. Baldar moved in, ducking from crate to crate, shooting at anything blue. He and the men moved from room to room, shooting as they moved. Men around Baldar told him what to watch out for, but he seemed to do well.

"Time!" said the man standing next to the TV.

Baldar paused the game and returned to Brent as another man took his place. "What is it you want, magus?"

"I was just wondering why you have armor."

Olron said with a laugh, "I could have told you why."

Baldar crossed his arms. "I was born that way."

"You can't take it off?"

"No. It is a part of me. Why do you care?"

"I was hoping we could, you know, get along better."

Still glaring at Brent with those white eyes, he said, "You created me. You can control me. I do not want to be controlled, not anymore. Is that understood, magus?"

Olron said, "He's not like your creator."

"All magi are like my creator."

"I promise I won't control you," said Brent, meeting Baldar's eyes.

Baldar merely glared back, unblinking. "You believe that, until you are tempted. All magi want power for their magic. That is what we are."

He pushed by Brent and went outside.

Brent watched him leave. "What was that all about?"

"A dragon is the purest expression of the magi's power," said Olron, also looking in that direction. "It's what we are."

Brent saw Shorty at his cot with some other guys, looking again at a laptop. Brent remembered something.

"I need to go back to the riders," he said to Olron. "They have something I need."

"I'll walk you there."

Brent walked side by side again with Olron.

"You generally like us humans," Brent said. "How come?"

Olron chuckled. Brent couldn't see his face in the darkness. "You're interesting. You change."

"Is that bad?"

"I don't think so."

Then the mortars started up again. They walked faster to the container at the HLZ. Inside, they heard the muffled thumps of return fire. He and Olron went to the riders' barracks.

"Hi," Brent said, coming inside.

The three women stood up. All wore their typical t-shirts and pants.

Brent saw what he was looking for at Jen's cot. "Can I borrow a laptop?"

Jen reached for hers. "You can borrow mine, sir."

"Brown-noser," said Meghan with a laugh.

Olron watched curiously as Brent took the laptop.

"It'll be just a few minutes. I want to check my email."

"Of course, sir."

There was a note from Lori, but he ignored it and the spam.

Hey, Doc—

he addressed to Dr. Arthur Bates.

What do you know about the Black Lions? They attacked me
back in Mass and here. They seem immune to magic. I thought
I was protected.

Brent

He skimmed the note from Lori. It went into how unfair the daycare was about Dante, and that she thought she was black-listed from all the daycares in Worcester. He didn't bother to reply.

He logged out and gave the laptop back to Jen.

"I may need it tomorrow or in a couple of days," he said. "I sent a very important email back home."

"Anytime."

Brent was tied up to a pole, not unlike someone who would get shot for treason. In his civvies, he stood before the colonel. His JAG lawyer was nowhere to be found. They were both inside a refrigerator, while the colonel sat at a counter. The refrigerator wasn't on, so it was hot. Brent sweated, though the colonel looked just fine.

His JAG lawyer had told him that he wasn't going to be court-martialed. Brent's information was dated, he said. Because Brent had spent most of his time in the field, he didn't know who was doing what anymore in the Magic Corps. But the colonel looked like a hardass.

Now that he was tied up, he knew the colonel was going to go after him.

"You were asked about the dragons," said the colonel. "What did you say?"

"Nothing, sir. I had no knowledge."

"And now?"

"I won't say anything."

The colonel turned from the counter to look directly at Brent. He had black eyes, bottomless. Brent did not look at him.

"You will tell me about the dragons."

The voice that came out of the colonel was Scar's. Brent risked a glance in the colonel's direction. Scar sat in the chair this time. Brent felt his blood run cold.

"Not this time," said Brent.

Scar only shrugged. "You wish to lose your manhood this time?" He rose, a long, wicked knife in his hand — almost as big as a scimitar.

"You won't win this time."

"How will you go home and fuck your girlfriend? Or any girl for that matter? Or any man?"

Scar approached Brent. Brent, surprisingly, was hard in his jeans. Scar unbuttoned the jeans, ticking down the zipper inch by inch. Scar parted the pants and Brent sprang out, pointing straight at Scar.

Scar touched the tip of the knife to the head of his cock. "You don't care? Then I will cut it off a bit at a time until you do."

Scar began sawing at his bulbous head, but it didn't hurt. He saw the blood flow onto the knife. It wasn't hurting; in fact, he was getting harder. He could feel the blood pulsing down there, but as for pain, there was none.

"How many dragons are there?"

"None."

Scar pulled a piece of flesh off the knife and held it before Brent. Brent kept his gaze at the door to the fridge. He thought he could hear blood dripping onto the floor. He smelled iron.

"What is their flight pattern?"

This time he touched the point of the blade to the exposed muscle that was cut away.

Brent couldn't look anymore and threw up.

He felt himself heave as he woke up. Fully clothed, he was tangled in the blankets and had fallen on the wooden floor. Marines slept around him. He felt his groin to make sure that all his parts were where they should be.

Brent sat up, blinking, his heart racing, tasting bile. He reached for his wooden staff and, using it for leverage, got up from the floor.

He went outside into the dark and saw a man at the dragon's tent, standing off to the side, looking out toward the barracks. He waved. Brent wasn't sure who it was but walked the few yards over to him. As he got closer, he could see the short black hair and glowing red eyes.

"Olron," said Brent. "What are you doing up?"

"I've slept enough," he said. "I would ask the same of you."

"Bad dream."

"Oh?"

"Post-Traumatic Stress Disorder, they said. But they still cleared me to come back."

"What does that mean, 'Post-Traumatic Stress Disorder'?"

"I had a traumatic experience and I'm stressed out by it."

Olron gracefully dropped to the ground, sitting cross-legged on the rug outside of the tent. "Tell me about it."

Brent, not so gracefully, sat down on the ground next to him. "I was kidnapped. Tortured. They wanted to know about dragons. At the time, I didn't know."

"But now you know."

He sighed. "Yeah."

"What happened?"

"I told them everything. In the military training, you're told not to tell them anything. But I sang like a canary."

"Was your life in danger?"

Brent rubbed his shoulder, the one the hook had been through. "They were tearing me apart. They beat me with a board with nails. They tore out my shoulder. I don't know how—"

"Did you use magic?"

"I couldn't. It would bounce back at me."

"Who did this to you?"

"The Black Lions. The ones I wrote an email to my friend back in the States."

"I haven't heard of them. I am most familiar with you humans, so I think I'd know."

Talking to Olron helped clear Brent's mind, making the dream shatter into pieces that he could label as a dream, and not memory.

He sat silently for a while, looking out at the starlight. The full moon would last another night, and then the wolves would change back into men — if they chose. The barracks were quiet; no howling tonight.

Olron touched Brent's leg. Brent looked sharply at him.

"What are you thinking about?" Olron asked.

"The wolves."

"Ah, yes. They're common here."

"We don't discriminate against the paranormals or humans. We have a 'don't ask, don't tell' rule."

"What does that mean?"

"If you're a paranormal, you don't have to tell the military. And we don't have the authority to ask you if you're paranormal."

"What if you say you are? Or, in the case of the lycans, you change?"

Brent shrugged. "Nothing happens, as far as I know."

He looked at Olron's hand on his leg. Part of him wanted Olron to move closer. Olron was handsome in the human form. He had his shirt off in the cold night air, displaying his perfectly formed pecs and abs, looked strong, and, most of all, human. What did Makrah say: that it was good to mate before battle?

Olron removed his hand. The warm area that he had touched suddenly grew cold. Brent let out a breath he didn't realize he was holding.

"Are you all right?" asked Olron.

"I'm better now, thank you."

Olron looked down at the ground. "I must have misread you."

"Misread me?" Brent caught Olron's eye.

"You looked in need of comfort, and humans like touch for comfort."

Brent looked down at his leg. "I did like that. I meant I was better after talking to you."

Olron replaced his hand on Brent's leg. Brent felt himself stiffen in his shorts. He couldn't do anything, not out here. He did not want to have the reputation of being a gay soldier. And besides, there was Chrissie to think about.

Olron did rub his hand up and down Brent's thigh. Brent thought back to Bates, how he would start an encounter doing the exact same thing. His body remembered, and he started to heat up.

"I know dragons mate, but do they mate with males?"

"Yes, some do. Makrah has been known to."

"Makrah? Really?"

"We don't put the same negative connotations that you do on it. It's a primal need."

"So it's just sex." Brent smirked.

"For some. For Tyrath, that's what it is. Though I believe that Sergeant Belliveau has a different perspective."

Brent swallowed. Olron stroked from his knee to his abdomen, not moving to his groin, and not moving inside his thigh.

"You think Meghan loves him?"

"Yes. I can tell by how she acts around him."

"How?"

"She hangs onto him."

"What does he do?"

"Tolerates it."

"You don't want to ... mate with Debbie? Or Jen?"

"How obvious do I have to be to show you who I would rather mate with?"

Brent shifted. He was fully hard now, not quite painfully, but he was uncomfortable. "It's just sex?"

Olron did get closer, his leg touching Brent's. Brent could have sworn that Olron's leg burned, was hotter than even Brent's skin, which already felt feverish. Brent, for his part, did not move.

"No," whispered Olron, moving his face close to Brent's.

Brent knew what was coming, and his hormones screamed. He wanted to pull Olron down, right here in front of the tent, tear off his clothes and fuck his brains out. Olron looked ready for it, his red eyes slowly closing, as he moved in closer.

The kiss was gentle, light, a brush of lips on lips. Brent opened his mouth to pant, and Olron closed his mouth on top of Brent's. Brent's nerves sang at the contact, as Olron's tongue — thick and long — slid along Brent's lips and into his mouth. Brent didn't know if he moaned, couldn't tell when his hand came up and cupped Olron at the back of the head and pulled him tighter. But when the kiss broke, so they both could breathe, his hand was entwined in Olron's thick black hair. His other hand was on Olron's chest, as if trying to both pull him in and push him away.

"Olron," said Brent breathlessly, "not here."

Olron was mere inches away from his face. "Too out in the open?"

Brent nodded.

Olron looked back at the tent. "There's a space that you can move here in this tent."

"What would the rest of the dragons say?"

Olron sat back, pulling away from Brent's hands. "Nothing."

"I don't think Baldar would be happy about it."

"Baldar needs to get over it."

Brent laughed softly. Olron merely sat next to Brent, their legs touching. Brent was still hard and hot, unsatisfied, but his rational mind had kicked into gear.

Olron said, "Think about it. Staying in our tent instead of with the riders would be better. We can guard you and make sure that you're not attacked by those Black Lions." He motioned to the container. "Who knows, maybe they can get into that building and kill you."

"If they were going to kill me, they would have done it before," said Brent. "They want to scare me, make me give them information."

"We dragons," said Olron seriously, "are protectors of magi. I swear by my blood that I will protect you."

Brent's chest swelled. He wanted to kiss Olron again but was afraid he would do more than kiss him. "I-I appreciate that. I'll think about it."

"I would really like to mate with you, Magus."

Brent gulped. "Did you mate with your creator?"

"I never had a chance. He died after creating me." Olron let out a small sigh. "He put all his energy and will into creating me, and he collapsed and died. I was out in the world. Then I met other dragons."

"You mean there's more than just you four?"

"Many more, Magus. In the mountains and the volcanos, in the desert and the ice caps, many dragons exist."

"I never would have thought."

Olron laughed. "You think dragons are a rare breed? We're everywhere."

"Why did you come out here? Now?"

"Makrah. He believes that the Taliban brings horror to the people. Makrah believes in democracy, that people should have a voice."

"Heh. He sounds like he's from America."

"He is actually a Roman dragon."

"As in ancient Rome?"

"Exactly that. He's the oldest of us all. He knew Caesar."

"Did he help Caesar?"

"I wouldn't be surprised if he did. You know the Romans did have dragons in their legions."

"It's not in any of the histories."

"Because histories are written by humans, not by dragons." Olron rose gracefully to his feet. "How long until patrol?"

Brent glanced at his watch. "Less than an hour."

"I will see you then," said Olron with a smile, and held his hand down for Brent to take it. Brent did, and Olron pulled him effortlessly to his feet.

The two stood there for a moment, holding hands, looking at each other's eyes. Brent couldn't tell what was behind those glowing red eyes, but Olron was smiling.

Brent let go, and Olron walked back into the tent.

Brent decided on a cold shower right about then.

At around 0200, he went to the HLZ to see Baldar set up. Deb waved at Brent, and Baldar dipped his head.

"Be careful, you two," Brent called up to them.

Deb carried the radio, a helmet with a microphone at her mouth. "Radio check," she said. She nodded, gave Brent a thumb's up. She patted Baldar's neck, and they took off into the air.

Brent went back to the TOC to get himself some coffee. He sat in the far back, away from the commotion. Sipping his coffee, he contemplated the usual organized chaos of the TOC.

The Ospreys containing contingents of Marines brought the troops to a helicopter landing zone south of a village in the Pesh valley. Reports were that Taliban were transporting weapons near there.

"Iceland in position," said a radio operator. "Awaiting orders."

"When our men are in position. They're running support."

Brent watched as a drone with a night vision camera highlighted the sleeping town. It was four hours before dawn.

The door to the TOC opened and Makrah, in casual fatigues and barefoot, stepped inside. The commander nodded to him.

"Ah, Wizard," he said, keeping his voice low. "You've come to watch the ice works?"

It didn't sound as good as "fireworks", but Brent smiled just the same. He offered Makrah his seat, but Makrah refused.

"If I sit, I will be lazy."

Brent chuckled. "You're a Marine, too."

"Is that what it means to be a Marine? Good, because I cannot swim."

They fell silent as the Afghan Army group with US support started getting into place in the green zone west of the village. They wanted to catch the Taliban sleeping.

The dragon covered any possible escape route though the crops. The Afghan Army went in, and every once in a while there would be a "sitrep" — a situation report — which one radio man would get, and report to the room at large.

By sunrise, no Taliban escaped through the crops, but the soldiers wondered about the *wadiz* — underground irrigation tunnels meant for water, but recently used for transport of men and materiel.

"Iceland requests permission to plug a *wadiz*." The radio man looked at the commander, who looked at Makrah.

"Copy, Iceland, it's a go."

"He means," said Makrah to Brent, "he will cover the hole with ice so no one can get out of it." Makrah smiled. "See? We can do more than terror."

Brent got up, put the chair in an out of the way place, and nodded to the door. Makrah looked confused for a moment, but realized he was to follow Brent out.

"Tell me what you can do," said Brent outside.

"Baldar and I can freeze running people or animals, sometimes even vehicles if they are slow enough. We can generate cool air, and, in the winter, create storms. We can also make it rain or mist."

"What about Olron and Tyrath?"

"They are destruction. There is nothing that can stand against them. We tested it on one of your old vehicles. Tyrath melted it."

"He melts rock," said Brent. He leaned against the TOC building. "How did you meet?"

"I knew Olron from a past life."

Brent looked confused.

Makrah said, struggling with the words, "A past time. We fought with another mage a long time ago. In China." He looked north. "Tyrath fought for the other side. Olron knew Baldar."

"Why did you come here?"

"We heard you are here to assist. To make these people great and united." He looked steadily at Brent, slitted blue eyes boring into him. "You are an army of war yet come here for peace."

"We're not here to wage war," said Brent spouting a line he had heard on the way to Afghanistan two years ago. "We're here to defend what's right."

Makrah nodded. "The Afghan people need freedom. And you, the United States of America, are all freedom."

"Makrah," Brent said, "you're an American dragon."

Makrah laughed, a deep resonant laugh. "Ah, Wizard. There are many dragons in your United States. I am not one of them."

Later that morning, after reveille, Brent watched the riders get mounted up with the dragons. Something came to him: What if the dragons themselves could have radios? They wouldn't need riders.

Makrah left last. The riders might be disappointed if they didn't have the dragons anymore, but they probably would be safer. And the dragons would be able to perform other feats without having to worry about if their rider would fall off.

Brent went to the TOC again. He introduced himself to the radio operator and asked for his commander. Sergeant-Major Proulx was a tall, thin black man, bald, with a wide face and an equally wide grin when Brent told him his idea.

"Headphones for dragons?"

"At least for a receiver," said Brent. "It's not like they can talk in their dragon form."

"Well, shit," said Proulx, turning to look at the pieces of radios and other communication devices set upon an assortment of tables, chairs, and any flat surface throughout the room-sized container.

"Will they take it?"

"I'll have to ask the leader first. But where he goes, they usually follow."

Proulx went to a tall audio speaker and studied it. "Yeah. Yeah, I think I could jury rig something."

As Brent left the radio operator's container, a man came running up to him. It was the corporal from yesterday, the one who mentioned the depot.

"Hey," Brent said.

The corporal, out of breath, said, "Lieutenant Colonel Schiffer ... looking for you."

"Shit," Brent muttered.

He followed the corporal to HQ, but Schiffer wasn't there. The head honcho of the base was looking for him, and that could not be good. What would he want with him? Was it the goats? Or the dragons? Or something else magically related?

Brent found the lieutenant-colonel walking back from the depot. He saluted while Schiffer snarled, "What's this about goats?"

Brent said, "Sir. I need them for the dragons. Why? Is there something wrong?"

"Some fucking Afghans showed up this morning with a dozen fucking goats."

"You didn't send them away, did you?"

Schiffer glowered. "We're not a fucking goat farm, Sergeant."

Brent hunched his shoulders. "Sir, I understand, sir, but we need those goats. If I don't placate the dragons, they'll turn on us." Brent motioned to the FOB spread out behind him. "All this will be a smoking, frozen ruin."

Schiffer grumbled. "I knew it was a bad idea to take them on."

"Were they always here, sir?"

"They were here when we got here. That blue dragon, the old man, he brought the other three."

"Lieutenant Waters? How did he get involved?"

Schiffer shrugged. "The old battalion commander of the 63rd knew him. Back to the goats."

"Yes, sir. I need them."

"This isn't a farm," he repeated. "Get only what you need for the day."

"Yes, sir." Brent saluted.

"Is it coming out of your pay?"

"Captain Tai said that there was a special fund for this. I was going to go see him some time today."

"Come with us back to HQ. You need to put in a requisition. You know how to do that, right?"

"I, um, no."

"Mitch," he turned to one of the sergeants walking with him. "Walk him through how to get a requisition for petty cash to get the goats."

"Yes, sir," said Mitch, a man younger than Brent and one rank below him.

The lieutenant colonel stormed back to HQ with Brent and Mitch following.

Half an hour later, Brent had some petty cash and orders that he could use five men to go with him to Gimblr or any other village to get animals for "the care and feeding of the Fifth Wing." It was early in the morning, but he wanted to get the goats first off, so he was able to get a truck to go to Gimblr.

This time, the men of the village were ready for him. He got four very healthy goats for a good price, telling the villagers to come back to the base in the late afternoon the next day and they would have an auction for another set of goats or sheep.

Depositing the men at the depot, he left the goats with some water at the dragon's tent. He went to the TOC and hung out there for most of the day, as drones showed the dragons at work. However, Tyrath had disappeared out of radio and drone contact twice already. He appeared in Kandahar province around 1500, and back in Kunar three hours later.

"He disappears like that a lot?"

Radio ops all nodded. "At least twice a day."

Brent frowned. "I'll have to talk to him." He went to check on the goats. One was gone, but blood lay across the sand and the other three animals looked terrified.

Later that evening, Brent went to Jen's cot to check on his email. Jen looked exhausted, but readily offered her laptop.

Brent —

Above is a website for the Black Lions. It's in Arabic, but the pictures may be helpful to you.

What I know about them is sketchy. They were established in the 8oo's after the conquest of Spain and Portugal by the Moors. They were considered an Army of God, extremists even within the Muslim community, in that they went after the supernatural and the magical Children of the Moon (though they weren't known as that yet). Supposedly they were immune to the charms of the supernatural and trusted only in Allah.

How they are immune is supposedly due to a tattoo or some marking on them, or maybe even a spell. We don't know what it is, exactly, because they also do everything they can to reclaim the body of a fallen comrade. It's believed they are human or converted Children.

I've attached a link to a scholarly paper about the history of the Black Lions for your perusal. Of course, in the paper, they are considered a superstition and not considered to be real in the modern day. Allegedly, when the Moors finally left Spain, they were considered destroyed.

Now with the growth of the Children in the armed forces and around the world, it's assumed that the Black Lions may become more prominent and more papers will be written about them. I will, of course, keep an eye out for you.

As for your protection, I had stated to you that the Middle East is in flux. This includes Afghanistan, even though it is not exactly the Middle East. Because of the preponderance of American forces there, many of the extreme right-wing groups of Islam are coming out of the woodwork to fight the Americans. This means you.

Your protection extends to the Americas under the Queen's control, and unfortunately, that is all. Everything else is up to you.

I will do what I can on this end, but I can't promise you anything.

Arthur

Brent sat back.

"Something wrong?" Jen asked.

"Something I didn't expect." He clicked on the link Bates provided. It was in Arabic, like he said, but he saw three pictures. All three were men in black, holding up a bloody head. The background was either desert or mountains. There were no bodies, so he couldn't tell if they were members of the armed forces or not.

Debbie came over to him. "What's that?"

"The men who tortured me," said Brent. He scratched at his shoulder. The stitches from the daggers were healing, which was good.

He felt Debbie and Jen step away. He expected that, after all.

When he left at night for chow, he was very wary, keeping his staff at the ready. He wondered if Olron was serious about letting him stay with them.

After dinner, he went to the dragon's tent and found them gathered outside.

"Tyrath," said Brent, "you keep going out of radio range."

"We go where the war is," said Tyrath. "You do not fight here."

Brent raised his eyebrows. "You think we don't fight?"

Makrah smoked his hookah, looking between Brent and Tyrath.

Tyrath crossed his arms. "You wait for people to tell you to fight."

"That's the way of war," said Brent, "to wait for the right time and then strike."

"We have destroyed many weapons from your Pakistan through the mountains. Now they are afraid of us."

"Which means they'll use even more complicated ways that we don't know to get the weapons here."

Tyrath huffed, muttered something in Russian, and stalked into the tent. Olron chuckled. Brent looked at Olron and then at Makrah. Makrah shook his head.

"Makrah," said Brent. "I wanted to ask. Can I stay here with you? The dragons?"

Makrah set his hookah down. Baldar stared at Brent as if he was crazy.

"You must not invade our areas."

"I won't. I promise. I swear."

Makrah looked at Olron and Baldar. "Why do you want to stay with us?" asked Baldar.

"I feel safer."

"Safer? With us and not your brothers?"

In human form, Baldar did not wear armor, but he looked more elegant than the other dragons. Baldar raised an eyebrow, tilted his head.

"Respect. I agree."

Olron said, "I agree."

Makrah nodded. "I also agree. There is an area in the rear of the tent that you may have as your own."

"You'll need something to sleep on," said Olron.

"I'll bring one of the cots from the barracks. Thank you."

Brent went to the container, retrieved a cot and his kit, and moved to the dragon's tent. There was no light inside the tent, so Brent summoned a mage light to show him the inside.

There was a corridor of brown canvas curtains to the side of him, four areas separated by curtains. At the end of the makeshift corridor was an area that followed crosswise along the back of the tent. It was about five feet wide by ten feet long, more than enough room for him to lay out his cot.

Olron helped Brent set up the cot. Brent sat down on it in the wan light of the mage light, dim because he was tired. He had fought for and gotten food for the dragons; he had an idea for the headphones. He had been up since 0200, and hadn't slept well the night before because of that attack. He wanted to sleep.

Olron stood around, looking at Brent's kit bag. "You have things you must carry around with you?"

Brent looked at the bag. "Yes."

"What if it falls into enemy hands?"

"If they can spell the bag open, they get to read the letters from my mom. And the Army's grimoires."

"You have a spell on it? How interesting."

Brent started getting undressed. It was hot in the tent without air conditioning and smelled of weed and cinnamon.

"Where are you from, Olron?"

"Colorado."

"Really? Are there a lot of dragons in Colorado?"

"Where there's mountains or forests, there's dragons."

"I'll have to keep that in mind."

"We're reclusive, and don't have a problem eating people who invade our caves."

Brent yawned, hoping that would give him a hint.

"Why do you come here, Wizard?"

"It's my job."

"Is that all we are to you? A job?" Olron stared at Brent.

"No," Brent admitted. "I want to see you thrive. I want to see you work toward your greatest potential."

Olron said, "Lieutenant Waters wanted to know about us. Don't you?"

"I'm getting bits and pieces. As with any relationship, you need to trust me, first."

Olron leaned over. "I trust you, Wizard."

Olron was very close, within Brent's personal space, his face mere inches form his own. Olron kissed him. Olron pushed further, and Brent found himself giving it back. Olron pulled back.

Brent asked, "Do dragons do this with each other to show trust?"

"No," said Olron, running a hand down Brent's chest. "Humans do."

"Did you do this with Lieutenant Waters?"

"He ran away before I could."

Brent laughed. All semblance of exhaustion was gone as he gazed at Olron's classical body. Brent reached up and cupped the back of Olron's head, pulling him down to his lips again.

Finally! Brent thought, as the clothes came off.

The cot was only so wide, so they ended up on the floor.

9

KUNAR PROVINCE

BRENT AND LIEUTENANT PROULX of radio ops dashed up to Makrah getting outfitted for the morning patrol.

Brent had fallen asleep in Olron's arms for about four hours. When Makrah got up to leave for the patrol, he paused where Brent lay and told them that he was leaving. Brent, embarrassed, disentangled himself from Olron

"Don't leave until I show up," said Brent to Makrah, as he got dressed.

Makrah looked amused at seeing Olron in Brent's area. Olron left Brent to get dressed.

As soon as Brent had his uniform on, he ran out to the radio ops and got Proulx and his equipment. They both carried a duffel bag as they headed up to the airfield. When they got there, Shorty stood beside Makrah while the saddles were made ready.

"Hold on," called Brent. "We've got something for Makrah."

Proulx took the bag from Brent. He pulled out a large round speaker, with wires leading from it into the backpack.

Proulx said, "Bend down, Makrah, so I can see if this fits."

Brent got some tie-downs from the other bag while Proulx fitted the speaker in Makrah's right ear, like a hearing aid. Proulx fed the wires from the speaker to the radio, which he mounted in the saddle with the tie-downs. Additional bungee cords went around the hearing aid to keep it in place. Proulx made sure the wire was long enough for Makrah to turn his head fully to the left.

Makrah shook his head violently.

"Easy!" yelled Proulx. "It's not made for that."

Makrah tilted his head. He shook it, bent down. With his tail, he drew a plus sign in the sand.

Shorty said, "Turn up the volume. It gets windy up there."

Proulx turned it up. Makrah rose to a sitting position and tilted his head as if to listen. He turned from them and launched into the air, kicking up dust.

After the dust cleared, Shorty sighed. "Well. I guess he won't be needing me anymore."

"We'll always need you, Shorty," said Brent, putting a hand on his shoulder.

Shorty laughed. "I better see if my kit still fits." He waved and headed back into base.

Brent watched Olron get fitted for the headphone. Part of him — the romantic part, he assumed — wanted to run up to him and yell, "Be careful!", but the soldier part of him was the one that prevailed, that watched impassively as Olron shook his head to make sure the earphone was on tight. He looked around to make sure it was clear, then he took off. Brent felt his heart lift with him.

"That's one mighty big dragon," said someone behind Brent.

Brent turned around to see two men, one blond with a video camera pointing at the retreating dragon and another Hispanic man standing next to him. He didn't know which one spoke at first.

"I'm sorry," Brent said, "But who are you?"

The man without the camera stepped forward, holding out his hand. "Andrew Rodriguez from CBS News. My camera man, Nate Leander."

"You're not going to show them on the news, are you?"

"Why not?"

"They're secret."

"A dragon in the US Army is secret?"

"Yes, and they're working with the Marines." Brent said, "I didn't know about them until two weeks ago. They've only been working here, near the Paki border."

"Where the hell have you been? There's been rumors of supernatural creatures of all sorts in the Army."

"Like what?"

"I'll tell you mine if you let me tell yours."

Brent wasn't in the mood to play games with a newsman. "Don't you think the American people need to know?"

"And some environmentalist or animal rights activist will say we're exploiting them."

"With all due respect, but who are you?"

"Their liaison."

"Are you a magus?" He motioned to Brent's wand patch.

Brent raised an eyebrow in surprise. This newsman knew more than some of the Army guys. "Yes," Brent replied. "If you'll excuse me, I need to find a vehicle to follow him."

"We have a vehicle."

Brent paused. He could possibly get more information out of Rodriguez if they rode together. Of course, Brent had information that they would want, too.

"All right," Brent said.

"Can I interview you?"

"As long as I can interview you."

"Fair enough," said Rodriguez.

Brent followed them to a 4x4 hard-topped square Mercedes. He got in the back seat behind Rodriguez, as Leander put his gear in the rear. The trunk had three cameras and other detritus of what Brent supposed was a news organization.

"How long have you been out here?" asked Rodriguez, after he settled in the shotgun seat.

Leander hadn't said a word yet.

"A year," Brent said, as Leander started the Mercedes.

"You look awful young for your rank."

"Our ranks in the Magic Corps are a little different. For example, we don't have corporal ranks. You jump from a private to a specialist. Of course, it depends on the branch you're in."

"I know you magi are spread out among the Forces. What rank are you in the Magic Corps?"

"I'm a First Magus." He peered forward. "You have a radio?"

"Yes. They set us up for the Hornets' frequencies."

Hornets was Company A's designation. "I need Company B," Brent said. "That's where the dragon is going to be."

"Want to go back?" asked Rodriguez.

"Maybe the Hornets will tell us what's going on," said Brent.

"Are we at least going in the right direction?"

"South."

Company B was deployed to a trail well-known for smugglers, insurgents, and other transport from Pakistan. Supposedly one of the Taliban upper echelon leaders was being transported to Pakistan in the next few days and they wanted to catch him.

Today, the dragon was a distraction from the airborne drones that littered the sky over villages and trails.

Leander drove along the path — really a dried up stream.

Brent asked, "My turn. What kind of 'creatures' are there in the Army?"

"Vampires. Werewolves. I met one fae in Iraq, but they seem to be rare and don't like talking about themselves."

"Fae? Really?" He had heard they existed but hadn't met one.

"Sure. There's a basilisk in Iraq too. And harpies."

"Seems like they're all in Iraq."

"That's where the action is."

Brent chuckled. "They haven't been here long enough."

"Nobody cares about these backwoods. If I report that there's a dragon here, I might get some press." He grinned. "More press means —"

Something exploded on Leander's side and sent the vehicle flying up in the air. The door blew into the truck across from Brent, stopping just inches away from him as if held back by a shield. The

4x4 tipped sideways in the air and crashed down on the passenger's side, sliding a few feet down the trail.

The 4x4 was still running. Brent couldn't believe he was alive as he turned his head to the left to see the cracked glass of the door, inches away from his face.

"Fuck! Everyone all right?"

"Leander!" yelled Rodriguez.

Brent undid his seatbelt and shoved at the door on his left. It didn't move, so Brent gave it a hard mental push. It flew out of the truck, landing with a *thunk* in the middle of the stream bed. He reached over and grabbed Leander's head. His fingers sunk into soft matter and his hands came away with blood.

"Shit," he said, knowing there was nothing he could do for him.

"Oh, my God, shit —"

"Rodriguez, can you move out of where you are?"

"My arm's broken, I think. I can't move it."

"I'll heal it outside. Come out this way."

Rodriguez held his arm close to his chest, and Brent could see the blood seeping through his shirt.

Rodriguez looked over to Leander. "Oh, fuck."

"Go, go! Don't look!"

"Shit," said Rodriguez, using one arm to try and haul himself out of the truck.

Brent gave him a mental push too, but a lot more gently to get him out. Rodriguez slid down the underside of the vehicle, hissing as he fell against the heated areas from the running vehicle. When Rodriguez got clear, Brent leaned over and shut off the truck. Brent climbed out next, jumping down.

Brent spared a glance at Rodriguez, who stood shaking in the middle of the dry bed. Brent searched out mentally for more IED's but didn't feel any.

"I'm so sorry," he said. "We were talking, and I wasn't paying attention."

Brent took Rodriguez' arm. Rodriguez winced. He put one hand on Rodriguez's shoulder and squeezed. "I'll heal your arm. Sit down, it'll be easier."

Rodriguez watched as Brent used his other hand to feel along Rodriguez's arm, sense the break, and heal it.

"When I lift my hand, it's going to hurt for a minute, then it'll be sore. Ready?"

Rodriguez nodded as Brent let go slowly. Rodriguez grunted at the pain, almost like a good Marine.

"Nate. What about Nate?"

"The truck still runs. We'll turn around."

"How are we going to get the truck back on four wheels?"

"Leave that to me."

Brent turned from Rodriguez and used a spell to lift the truck off the ground. He turned it in the air, and the body of Leander tipped out of the truck, onto the dust of the dry bed. The side of his face was a bloody mess, down to his shoulder and arm hanging by a strip of flesh to his torso. Rodriguez swallowed and dragged Leander to the middle of the road as Brent set down the truck a few feet away.

"We'll put him in the way back," said Brent.

Rodriguez nodded. With a spell, Brent lifted the body, and placed him head-first, lying down across the trunk.

Rodriguez knew he was going to have to sit in a puddle of blood in the drivers' seat, but he used a jacket to try to clean it as best as he could.

"I think he's married," Rodriguez said. "I think he has kids."

"I'm sorry."

Brent watched Rodriguez wipe down the seat. The chair rocked as he wiped at it — the front screws holding it down had let go. Rodriguez ended up smearing blood across the seat. He tossed the jacket on the floor in the back and got into the truck. Brent got in the passenger's side. He had to climb in through the window.

Rodriguez got the truck into first gear. The truck didn't get out of second gear, so they drove slowly back to FOB Blessing. At a checkpoint, two kilometers from base, the two men showed their IDs. The sentries looked in the rear and waved them through.

Brent helped take out the body. A chaplain walked over to them after seeing Brent and some Marines with the body.

He asked, "What religion was he?"

"I never asked," said Rodriguez. "We started working together in Iraq. He wasn't religious."

The chaplain said, "We'll take care of him."

"Okay," said Rodriguez.

Four Marines men took the body, as Brent stood with Rodriguez. "You going to be all right?"

"I have to call the office."

Brent nodded. "Let me know if you need anything."

"Yeah, thanks."

Rodriguez walked away from the truck, leaving it parked in the middle of the base. Brent pushed it to the side using his magic.

He knew he wasn't going to get a ride anywhere, so went to the TOC. The first lieutenant there shook his head. Something was going on, and he would be in the way.

It was starting to get hot outside, so in the tents it would be really hot. *Well, when you get lemons …*

He went back to his tent, got some paper and pens, and went to the mess hall which was cooler. He wrote letters to Chrissie and his family, except Keithy. He partially blamed Keithy for what happened at his party when he was captured, so that was the last severing stroke between them, as far as he was concerned.

He took a shower, luxuriating in the cold water on a hot day, even though, as soon as he stepped out, he got dust all over his body, smearing the red dirt on himself as he dried off.

Hi Chrissie,

A man died on my watch today. This really isn't the first time it's happened. Just a few days ago, one of my old teammates died. I had taught him a bad habit.

Death is part of war, I guess. I don't like it if I can prevent it, though I'm a healer in addition to being a scout—a defender as well as offense. We have some magi that are necromancers. They can raise people from the dead. They don't do it to our soldiers, and I don't think they're allowed to do it with people. I don't hang out with that crowd. Our SO said that it takes a special kind of cold-hearted person to be a necromancer.

I'm beginning to become friends with the members of the Fifth Wing

"Sergeant Rogers?"

Brent looked up from his writing. He sat alone in the chow hall. "Hello, Chaplain," he said to the man who spoke.

"Call me Harry," he said. He looked around the room. "Can I join you?"

"Sure." Brent put aside the pad and pen and made room for him on the bench. "Checking on me?"

Harry was an older man, as most Army chaplains seemed to be. He had salt and pepper hair, sparkling black eyes, He stood as lean as any grunt, but was not as buff — but he wasn't as loose as a rear echelon desk jockey. He wore a gold cross with a line through its top.

Brent said, "I've never seen that kind of cross before."

"Oh, this." He held it up. "Russian Orthodox Christian. We're close enough here. I thought I'd study it." The chaplain sat. "I know you're a sapper."

"Yes," said Brent. "I wasn't paying attention this time."

"Are you going to be all right?"

Brent shrugged. "If it was my team, it would be different. I barely said two words to the guy." Brent rubbed his hand on his thigh, the hand that had touched the man's brain.

"If you need to talk about it, let me know."

"I've seen dead people before, sir."

"It's worse for the doctors and the healers sometimes."

"I'm not quite guilt-ridden."

Harry rose. "Okay, then. You have today off?"

"I can't really do anything. TOC is busy and I need a vehicle to chase a dragon."

"Most people want to run away from them."

"I need to make sure they're doing what they're supposed to do."

"Are they?"

"Most of the time."

"What do you do if they don't?"

Brent looked at his hand on the table. "I hope I never have to find out, sir."

Although Brent was tired, he summoned up the will to take himself to the gym. Olron and the dragons probably wouldn't understand the need for a workout, and he had been long overdue.

The gym had the usual weights. Typically, a few Marines would be outpacing themselves in friendly competition.

Brent found Jen at the rowing machine. She smiled and waved at him, pausing for half a second, then started rowing again. He settled down with some weights.

He hadn't done this in a while, so had to build himself up bit by bit. He didn't notice when Jerry had come in to take the spot next to him.

Brent looked at the arm he had healed the first day he showed up. It looked fine, muscles working under the skin. He was proud of himself that he had done such a good job. Brent nodded to Jerry, but he had eyes only for Jen.

She smiled at Brent, got off the rowing machine.

Jerry stood up. "Hey," he said.

She turned to him, looked him up and down, and wrinkled her nose. "Hey."

"Whachu doin' after this?"

"Take a shower and go read."

"We could take one together."

She sighed. "No."

He approached her. "C'mon, baby."

She raised an eyebrow. "Baby?"

Said Brent from his bench, "The sergeant said 'no'."

Jerry didn't even look at Brent. "Stay outta this, man."

"She's above you and she's a Marine. You don't want to fuck with her."

Jerry ignored Brent, talking to Jen, "C'mon. You'll enjoy it."

"I doubt that," she said.

She walked by him with an "Excuse me," to Brent, and left the gym.

Jerry started to follow, but Brent raised a hand and, using his will, pushed him sideways into the wall so hard that it rattled.

"Da fuck —"

He tried to get away from the wall, but Brent held him there. Jerry looked around in a panic and saw Brent, his hand up at his waist, glaring at him.

"You gonna leave her alone?"

"*You're* doing this?"

"Yes. You going to leave her alone?"

Jerry squirmed. "Jesus Christ, man, let me go."

Brent motioned with his hand and Jerry stumbled away from the wall, almost falling. He caught himself on the weight rack.

"I'm holding you to it," Brent warned him, walking out of the gym.

10

FOP BLESSING

BRENT STOPPED OFF at the riders' container — although they were no longer riders. Debbie's hand was bandaged up.

"What happened?"

Debbie didn't say anything, but Jen said, "She got into a fight."

"Let me see," said Brent.

"No. I don't need a healing. I'm Catholic," said Debbie.

Brent said, "As far as I know, the Pope never came out one way or the other about magic."

Debbie shook her head. Brent shrugged, though inwardly he was disappointed. He wanted to help her feel better, but he understood and accepted her choice.

"Where's Meghan?" asked Brent.

"Tyrath didn't want a radio," said Debbie.

Brent said, "Gee. I wonder why."

Jen said, "I heard a drone spotted them in the mountains."

"Flying?"

"No, on the ground."

Brent sighed. "I'm going to have to talk to him."

★   ★   ★

He met with the TOC after the dragons returned.

The lieutenant in charge of the TOC pulled Brent aside. "Tyrath is still unreliable. If you won't talk to him, then we're going to talk to both of them."

Brent wasn't sure how to talk to Meghan without being a hypocrite. However, he wasn't doing it during work time. In times like these, he usually went down to the range and popped off a few hundred rounds. That kind of mindless work helped him clear his mind so he could be inspired.

An exposed area off to the south of the barracks, facing the base of a mountain, the range's area ground was decorated with holes caused by some mortar shells from the mountain.

A platoon in prone position shot at stationary paper targets. Brent watched them while he leaned on his staff.

"Afternoon," said a man whose name in big block letters spelled out 'KROFF' above the left pocket of his tunic. He motioned to the staff Brent carried. "Going to shoot things with that?"

"I was hoping to borrow a rifle first."

"Here." Kroff handed over his assault rifle. "Or you can use magic."

"I'd blow the targets to smithereens." Brent smiled. "It doesn't exactly have a power control."

"Aren't you the power control?"

"With me, it's all or nothing."

A couple of men got to a standing position. Brent had won most of his marksman medals from that position. He hefted the AR, waiting for someone to clear a spot on the range.

Brent stepped into line behind the shooters. After everyone finished firing, some went downrange to check on their targets. Men smoked and bullshitted while they waited. When they returned, targets in hand, new targets had been put up in their place. They were all silhouettes of a man with a raised knife.

Brent took aim at the torso. Someone started shooting, and then Brent squeezed the trigger. His body rocked with the first few shots, not used to the length of the trigger on the rifle. He stood wider and took more shots.

"Hold!" yelled a man, and everyone aimed their rifles down.

A man with binoculars came over to Brent's side and looked out at his target. "You got him in the chest a few times."

"That's what I was going for," said Brent.

The man nodded. "Most of these guys go for the head, but the torso's a bigger target."

"Yes, sir," said Brent.

"Down!" someone yelled, and everyone dove to the dirt, aiming their guns downrange. Brent settled in, the butt of the rifle against his shoulder. He aimed for the lower torso this time.

"Fire!"

The gun jumped, almost hitting his cheek, and would have broken it. He felt the familiar thrust of the gun against his shoulder as the bullets fired, hot casings flying off to the side onto the ground. When everyone finished their magazine, they stumbled to their feet.

Brent found Kroff to return the rifle before heading down the hundred yards to the end of the range.

A young kid asked him, "How come you don't have a rifle?"

"Can't carry a magic staff and a rifle," said Brent, holding up his paper target. Most of the shots got the torso. None got the head.

"What happens if you use that staff?"

Brent went behind the hay bales that served as a stopgap for the bullets. He pulled out a fresh paper target and attached it to two nails on the hay bales. "You'd be less one set of hay bales."

"We can get more," said another guy.

Brent laughed as he walked back.

"C'mon, bro, I ain't seen a wizard in action."

"Fine, fine."

"Cool!"

At the firing line, Brent waited for the command to let loose. The man studied Brent, who nodded "ready" at him.

"Fire!"

Brent pulled the spell for lightning and aimed it at the target. A bolt of energy erupted from the top of the staff. He felt the energy jerk out of him, out of the crystal tip of the staff, flying across the range to the hay bales. The bolt of energy exploded the paper target and the hay bales behind it, sending a shower of hay and confetti across the two targets on either side.

"Holy shit!" was the most common exclamation when Brent set his staff back down on the ground.

"You do that to people?" asked Kroff.

"It's been a while," said Brent.

He remembered when he was first stationed in Afghanistan, with Custer and his team. On their third day out, Brent took out a sniper — and the entire floor of the building he was shooting from. Brent didn't mean to, but he was scared.

"Don't let me get on your bad side, man."

"Thanks for letting me use your rifle."

"Sure."

Brent left the range, heading toward Meghan's barracks.

No one was there. At the dragons' tent, Makrah sat outside.

"Makrah, I have a favor to ask."

"Of course, Magus."

"Could you talk to Tyrath?"

"What about?"

"He can't keep disappearing like he does. We lose track of him. He keeps destroying villages that don't need to be destroyed."

"You must understand, Magus, that he is a battle dragon."

"I know that. But can't he wait —"

"Battle dragons have one function: battle. If you cannot give them battle, then they will find it themselves."

"He'd find plenty of battle if he wore the radio."

"Yes, probably."

"Why doesn't he wear it?"

"He is an old battle dragon," said Makrah. "Change does not come easily to the old."

Finally, Brent caught up with Meghan. After Tyrath went into his tent, a woman tried to sneak toward the riders' container.

"Sergeant Belliveau," said Brent, standing in the doorway of the container. His mage light gave dim blue color to her face.

She stopped short.

"Mind if we talk?"

"Of course not, sir," she said.

"What were you doing with Tyrath this late?"

"Talking."

"About?"

She shrugged. "Things."

"Your tunic is off a button."

Meghan looked down. She fumbled with it, having to undo most of it.

He watched her re-button the shirt, and said, "Having sex with a member of the opposite sex in any way is against regulations, Sergeant."

"What makes you think we're having sex?"

He motioned to her shirt. "I doubt you were like that all day, unless you got dressed in the dark."

She crossed her arms and glared at him.

"Then explain to me why you keep disappearing out of range."

"We go where the action is, sir. There's smuggling in the Pesh Valley, Taliban are streaming over the border, and here we are building schools and giving pens and toys to kids, and we're not fighting!"

"We have to win their hearts and —"

"Minds. That's what the president said, but he's not here, is he? He doesn't see what's going on. We need to *destroy* the Taliban, grind them into dust and salt their graves."

"Is that what Tyrath says?"

She shrugged. "Sometimes."

Brent crossed his arms. "You're going against direct orders. You and Tyrath have a flight path. You're not supposed to go into the other provinces and destroy any village you find."

"If you've paid attention to what we've been doing, *sir*, you would notice that we've been going after villages that have been Taliban strongholds."

"Under what intelligence? Who told you they're Taliban strongholds?"

"They're in the mountains. Or on the valley floor. They're smugglers' havens."

"I asked you who told you?"

"It's well known, sir."

"How long ago?"

Brent saw the look of rage cross her face for a moment before becoming a soldier's emotionless mask.

"Before doing this, I was a drone maintenance operator. I was in the TOC and I saw first-hand what we couldn't do. Then the dragons came. You might have Olron and Makrah wrapped around your little finger, but Tyrath isn't like them. Tyrath fights, and so do I."

Brent said, "I'm going to have to remove you."

"What?" She dropped her hands to her hips, her emotionless mask disappearing into one of shock.

"Sorry, but they have their own radios, and we don't need to endanger you any longer. Any questions?"

Very quietly, almost a whisper, she said, "No, sir."

He nodded once, and went back to the dragons' tent, taking his mage light with him.

Olron stepped out of his curtained-off area. Brent didn't know what his collection was, and, as he had promised, didn't look in anyone's area.

Olron closed the curtain and turned to Brent. "Did you see her?"

"Yes."

"Did you talk to her?"

"Yes."

"And?"

"I need to talk to Tyrath."

"I heard my name," grumbled the dragon from his curtained-off spot next to Olron's. Tyrath opened the curtain. He was naked.

Brent snapped his head up to look at Tyrath's slitted blood-red eyes.

"I'm going to ask this once. Are you and Sergeant Belliveau having sex?"

Tyrath tilted his head.

Olron said, "Mating. Are you two mating for pleasure?"

Tyrath looked at Brent, then looked at the mage light. "Yes." Tyrath said.

"Dammit," spat Brent. "She's lying."

"She does not call it mating."

"What does she call it?"

"'Making love.' Is there a problem?"

Tyrath looked from Brent to Olron, who said, "She wants to be your permanent mate."

"Impossible," said Tyrath.

"Do you think you could tell her that?" said Brent. "Because she's probably head over heels in love with you."

"I will tell her tomorrow. I cannot be her permanent mate. It is pleasure, nothing more."

Someone was going to have a broken heart.

A couple of days later, Brent got out of the TOC again and, this time, he was able to go with a group to follow Olron's flight path. After their normal landing in the wee hours of the morning, waiting around for the ANA to show up after dawn prayers, the men were supposed to head to an orchard, just to their east. They were close enough to the Paki border that they could probably throw an RPG over it.

There were no villages, so there should have been no people in the area. Their objective was to clear the treeline.

The Black Cat company Brent travelled with today walked across a plain heading right toward the group of trees. As he half-expected, a shot rang out, then many shots, and he dove to the ground, slamming his face in the dirt. He turned to his left to see a man firing with his rifle toward the trees.

"Shit," someone spat.

Brent looked to his right. Almost on top of him was an infantryman, setting up his Semi-Automatic Weapon, a large gun with a band of bullets attached.

"Hold this," he said to Brent, handing him the band, feeding it into the gun.

The sound of the SAW deafened Brent, since he wasn't used to being this close to one. Its rattle was like loud booms in his ears. He thought he could hear the *zip-ping* of ricocheting bullets.

Someone was calling for Cinder Two. Brent raised his head and looked across the plain. The SAW stopped shooting, and the soldier dug out another belt of bullets.

"Got it now. Thanks, man." He started loading the belt into the SAW.

"Don't mention —"

He started shooting, drowning out any other words Brent might have said.

Above the noise, Brent heard the roar of the dragon. A primal sound, one of a predator that hunted people, it made the hair on the back of his neck stand on end and gave him goose-bumps. He looked in the direction the noise came from, on their side of the border, heading north to south, aiming directly for the trees.

The group of trees took up a relatively small area, probably about two kilometers north to south, and one kilometer from east to west. Brent heard the gunfire ease, as Olron, the red dragon, came swooping out of the sky, his wings wide, his body thin and lithe. He roared again, much closer this time, and the soldiers around him raised their heads.

"Shiiit," said the infantryman next to Brent.

"Yeah," whispered Brent, as his heart leapt in pride. He couldn't help but grin.

Olron banked, as if hitting an invisible barrier, and came down on the trees. He opened his mouth and bright red flame shot from it, saturating the treetops, the ground, and everything between. They could hear the *whoosh* of the fire from the living flamethrower,

The north side was engulfed in flame. Olron twisted and rose up in the air, then came at the treeline from the south. He did the same thing, roar before firing, warning those who dared to remain that he was going to be the last thing they heard before burning to a crisp. Again, red and orange flame slammed into the trees, toppling them while they caught fire, the sand itself probably melting under the heat.

Olron then swooped up in the air with a roar of triumph, echoed by the men on the ground around Brent.

Brent found himself yelling along with them.

11

FOP BLESSING

T HE SEALS WALKED IN like they owned the place. SEAL Team 3 arrived on September 18 at 0300. After arriving at the base, the men took up residence in the container that Brent had been in. He was glad that he had moved out to the dragons' tent because he even knew that Marines and Navy combined did not end well. Although there might be friendly competition, there may be some long-lasting rifts created, and Brent didn't want to be in the middle of that drama.

As he watched the dragons leave in the early morning light, a mage light hovering over him, two men came over to him. One had a Navy tattoo on his forearm; the other man didn't have any tattoos that he could see. That one was so broad in the shoulders that he looked like a triangle. He was bald, and Brent saw his eyes: translucent gray of the vampire. The younger one with the tats still had his hair, though it was cut short, and he was fully muscled and well-defined.

"Good morning," said Brent.

"Mornin'," said the big man. "They're fucking huge."

"I didn't think they existed," said the younger man.

"Oh, they exist."

"They must eat a shitload of dog food," said the big man. He turned to Brent. "I'm Jack."

"Brent."

"Jamie," said the young man. "You always come to see them off?"

"I'm their liaison. Or lackey. Same difference."

Jamie chuckled. Jack smiled. "You're the wizard," Jack said. "The Queen's Wizard."

"You know about that?" Brent looked at his nose, not at his eyes.

"Everybody who's anybody does. We heard you got attacked back in the States."

"And here." Brent frowned. "How long are you guys here for?"

They looked at each other.

Jack shrugged. "I have to go find out. It's a week as it stands now, but this is war. Things can change."

"One thing I've learned in this job is to be flexible."

Jack nodded. "What do you do? Fog of war shit?"

"Some offensive stuff, though I've been mostly a healer these days."

"You like it?"

"We had a wizard," said Jamie at the same time.

Brent turned to Jamie. "What happened to him?"

"He got shot in the leg. He's in Germany now. He might get sent home."

"He was FOW," Jack said.

Brent nodded. One of the things they tried to teach him was piercing the so-called "fog of war" — that is, predicting what was on the other side of the hill. Some of the better magi could predict what the enemy was going to do. He knew the spells, they were in his grimoire, but he never memorized them because he knew that he wasn't built for the mental strategy of war.

Brent said to Jack's question, "I do like it."

"You ever get hit?"

"Not really. I have a personal field."

"What's your range?"

"For what?"

"The field."

"An entire Humvee, about two feet out. I can't put one on a person at a distance, though. That's a whole other magic system."

"You gotta touch the person?"

"Yes."

Jamie said, "Ray was like that, too."

"He had a field?"

"No. He had to touch a map for FOW."

"Some people are like that. Some people have visions."

"I wouldn't trust the visions," said Jack. "Could mean anything."

The dragons got ready to lift off. The men went silent as they watched Makrah leave first, leaping up into the air and swimming through it to gain altitude. Baldar was next, his ice white wings stretched out as he jumped up, making a small tornado of sand as he jumped. Tyrath followed, his squat body like a lizard's rising up as he flapped his wings. Olron ran and leapt, his wide red wings encompassing the area that all the dragons had been in, and he banked over Brent. Brent waved. The dragon tipped his wings back, as he flew over Brent and the two vampires.

"Wow," said Jamie, watching Olron fly into the night.

"Yeah," said Brent. He hoped they couldn't see his blush in the mage light.

"Where you off to now?" asked Jack.

"Probably going to get a cup of coffee. You?"

"Gonna check the HQ to find out if there's any meals to be had."

Brent knew that HQ had a list of people who would volunteer themselves for the vampires in the platoon. He had always registered for that list, but no vampires had ever come to him in the three years he'd been in the Armed Forces. Most times, vampires had people in their platoon they had a feeding relationship with, so the list was hardly ever used. Brent knew also that the feeding relationship could be intimate, like it was with Dr. Bates, or totally platonic.

His body reacted differently, though. The ecstasy that he felt by being fed from always threw his hormones into overdrive. He didn't know how he would react with this big guy feeding from him, and what the guy would expect.

"I, um, I'm on the list." Brent brushed his hands over his shirt.

Jack turned to Jamie. Jamie shook his head. "Age before beauty," he said.

"Fuck you," said Jack with a grin. "Any place private?"

"Follow me," said Brent, trying to keep his gait solid as he walked to the dragons' tent.

When they got there, he said to Jamie, "You wait out here. Don't go inside, okay?"

"Sure thing," said Jamie, standing guard outside. Brent pulled open the tent door and let the mage light head in first.

"Don't look in the other rooms," said Brent.

"Gotcha," said Jack, following Brent to his cot.

Brent unbuttoned his shirt. He looked at Jack, who stood and looked around the room. "You need a chair and a desk, Brent."

"I don't rate such a thing. Besides, I spend most of my time at the TOC."

Jack nodded. "Have you done this before?"

"It's been a few years."

"So you know what'll happen."

Brent swallowed and sat down on the cot. "Yeah."

"I can't help you with the reaction," said Jack, sitting down next to Brent. The cot almost tipped over toward Jack, so he sat closer to Brent. "I don't swing that way."

"I understand," said Brent. "Totally platonic."

"Totally," said Jack, leaning toward Brent's neck.

Brent tipped his head. He didn't feel any breath on his neck, as Jack didn't have to breathe. Jack put his arms around Brent to hold him still. Brent's heart beat faster in anticipation.

Jack licked at the area on his neck, applying venom that acted like a local anesthetic. Brent felt the pinch of the fangs, then the tear of flesh as the hole in his jugular grew bigger. His body stiffened, tried to pull away, but Jack held him tight.

Brent's heart beat fast, as the combination of the vampire's venom mixed with his blood and went right to his brain. Brent felt the anesthesia of the venom fill his mind with a high, not unlike heroin. Dr. Bates had explained that the venom reacted with dopamine and other hormones to give him the ecstatic and heightened arousal. In the middle of the moment, he didn't care.

He thought he could hear a moan at one point. Jack was definitely old, but not as old as Bates, because Brent was still aware of his surroundings, and the venom wasn't as powerful as to cause him to masturbate in front of Jack, like Bates could do.

Brent felt his body tip, lying on the cot now. His arms came away from Jack, as they had also wrapped around him, holding him close. Brent took a few deep breaths, trying to calm himself, though his heart had stopped racing. His cock was painfully hard under his pants, and he tried to ignore it.

He opened his eyes to darkness.

"You okay?" asked Jack.

Brent nodded. He went to sit up, and Jack helped him.

"Easy there, kid," said Jack. "I fed a lot."

His brain was a little foggy, and the mage light had gone out. Jack handed him a candy bar from one of the MRE rations.

"Thanks, man," said Brent, unwrapping the candy.

"Take it easy a few. You don't have to go anywhere right now, do you?"

Brent shook his head as he ate the candy. It would take maybe fifteen minutes before he was back to normal. That included his hard dick.

"Sorry," Jack said, "but it was a couple of days since I had a willing partner." Brent could tell the age of him by the use of "partner". Bates always called Brent a "companion."

"Nobody in your platoon?"

"Oh, sure, but they have to be in tip-top shape themselves, ya know? And a couple of the guys get squeamish."

Brent heard him move around. Vampires could see just fine in the dark, so he wouldn't be bumping into anything. Brent summoned the mage light again. It appeared as a round sphere that hovered over Brent's cot and bathed the area in a dim blue glow.

"You got scars, I noticed."

"I did this a lot when I was younger."

Jack nodded. "You think you'll be okay?"

"I will."

"Okay. I'm gonna see if Jamie's wants anything. He's been without it for at least three days. Even though he's only a 1960s baby, he still needs some sustenance."

"Right," said Brent, straightening himself out. He reached for his shirt.

"Oh, before I forget," said Jack. "I understand that we're supposed to protect you if we see you. Do you go out in the field?"

"Sometimes."

"Let us know if you need an escort."

"I've been fine so far."

"Yeah, but those Black Lions are out for you guys."

"How do you know about them?"

"They've been around for years. They're the Islamic version of the Inquisition. Not that I know anything first-hand about the Inquisition."

"You're not that old!"

He chuckled. "I knew Samuel Adams in passing."

"Ah." Brent pulled on the shirt. "I'll see the two of you later, then?"

"Where you going after mess?"

"TOC."

"See you there."

Brent found out that Jack was a lieutenant, Jamie a gunnery sergeant, and both of them were on the SEAL team that was here for R&R, such as it was.

He had to do his usual auction for animals at the entrance to the base at 1400 hours. The two vampires appeared out of nowhere while Brent was walking to the front entrance. Although it was overcast, the two vampires wore hats, black long-sleeved shirts and pants. They wore full face masks at their belts, just in case the sun burst through.

"You look good, Jamie." He had the pink skin of a human, which happened often to young vampires when they fed well.

"I had a good partner," he said. "So did Jack, I see."

Brent looked at Jack's huge arms to avoid looking him in the eye.

Jack chuckled. "Where are you headed?"

"I have to get the dragons' dinner." He held the Pashtun stone in one hand. "We have an auction every afternoon. The locals bring their animals."

"Healthy or not?"

"The dragons don't seem to care as long as they're alive."

"What kind of animals?"

"Sheep, mostly goats."

At the entrance, the guards nodded to them and let them through. At the major's orders, they held the auction a few yards away from the entrance so they wouldn't clog traffic.

Brent saw that a couple of new people had showed up with scraggly goats, so he approached them first. Jamie was talking to one man while Jack examined a couple of sheep. Brent stopped and watched the two vampires, acting and talking like regular human beings.

Jack pulled out a couple of sheep. "These look like the best of this group."

"Okay," said Brent, and Jamie started haggling.

Brent usually paid whatever they asked. But haggling was a minor sport in Afghanistan, and Jamie played it well. He got both goats for ten U.S. dollars.

Meanwhile, Jack found a couple of goats from two other men. Jamie switched to them and spoke in Pashtun.

One man looked disappointed, saying, "You Americans pay whatever we ask."

Jamie explained, "I'm here now, and I know how you work. If you don't want to negotiate, then we can leave it here, because there's plenty more than what you have."

The man grumbled and Jamie talked him down to five dollars. The other man was more obstinate, getting seven for his goat. Jamie left it to the Afghans to fight among themselves about how they would handle things, as Jack picked up a goat under each arm like they were footballs.

Brent tied up the goats at the dragons' tent. "Well, that was the highlight of my day."

"You just leave them out here?"

"They've never run away before." He put down some water and grass from a bale that he kept for that purpose behind the tent.

"You fatten them up for the dragons," said Jamie, watching.

"No, not really. But I hate leaving them out here without anything to eat or drink. Sometimes they don't come back for hours."

"When do they usually come back?"

"1900 or so. Baldar comes back earliest usually."

"Which one's which?"

"At 2000, I'll introduce you."

"Cool."

At 1928, Brent left mess to go to the dragons' tent. Outside, in the dark, with a lantern on the ground between them, Makrah smoked the hookah and Olron lay out lazily on a rug, reading a thick paperback book. Tyrath and Baldar were nowhere to be seen, but that wasn't unusual.

Makrah lifted his head. "I smell the dead on the wind."

"That would be us," said Jack, coming out of the dark.

Makrah's nostrils flared. He looked from Jack to Jamie to Brent. "You know these dead men?"

"They just got here this morning."

Olron put aside his book and got up. "I'm Olron," he said, holding out his hand.

"Jack."

"Jamie."

They both shook his hand.

"Which dragon are you?" asked Jack.

"The big red one," Olron said with a smile, winking at Brent. "The little red one is Tyrath."

"He didn't look so little to me," said Jamie.

Olron laughed. "Compared to me, he's little." He motioned to the rugs. "Come and sit."

Jack motioned to the hookah. "They let you have one of those?"

"No one has said otherwise," Makrah said.

"Where you from?" asked Olron.

"St. Louis," said Jamie quietly. He seemed to be awestruck at the two men.

"Boston," said Jack.

"I've never been to St. Louis," said Makrah. "I have been to Boston twice."

"I'm from Massachusetts too," said Brent. "Worcester."

"Worcester is where everyone went after the Great Burning in 1954," said Jack.

"The Great Burning?"

"After the war when McCarthy started going after the paras and the Communists. Paras were chased out of the big cities into the smaller ones. Some of us were staked. I could probably count them all on one hand, though."

"You know, I was wondering, why didn't the paras fight during the civil rights movement?"

"Because the paras knew that laws for civil rights should be for one minority group at a time. We can talk politics some other night," Jack said with a smile. "Do you have a name?" he asked Makrah.

"I am Makrah," he said. He didn't move to shake hands.

"He's our leader and guide," said Olron. "We have two others: Baldar who's a blue dragon and none too happy to be in human form, but they didn't have a tent big enough for him. Tyrath's around somewhere."

"Is he with Meghan again?" asked Brent.

"No," said Olron. "I think the last time you spoke to him about her, he got scared enough to break off the partnership."

Jack tilted his head. "Partnership?"

Olron said, "Mating practice."

Jack laughed.

Jamie stared at Olron, who turned to him. "I didn't know dragons could shape shift."

"We can, with help," said Olron. "My creator didn't give me the ability to do it, so I had to learn myself."

"Help how?"

"Magic," said Olron, and pointed to the ground. "There's magic not far from here."

"Olron," said Makrah sharply.

Olron glanced up at him, then looked humbly at the ground. Brent studied the two for a moment. Makrah seemed to have an aura about him, chilly to the vampires. Olron was friendly enough with the vampires; all of them were paranormals, supernaturals, Children of the Moon, weren't they?

Makrah picked up his hookah and went into the tent without saying another word. Jack and Jamie watched him leave.

"What was that about?" asked Brent.

"I don't know," said Olron, rising and gathering his book. "But that usually means I'm supposed to follow." He nodded to the three men and went inside.

Brent shrugged when Jack turned to him. "Sorry."

"He must have had a bad experience," said Jack.

"Does dragon's blood —"

Jack whirled on Jamie. "Don't you even think about it. They're paras like us. We don't feed from paras, remember?"

"Some don't," said Brent.

"*We* don't," reiterated Jack firmly. "You don't know what a para's blood will do to you."

"They say faery blood gets you high."

"We don't need to get high." He rose gracefully from the rug. "Tell Olron thanks. Do you need us to stay by you?"

"No, I'll be all right, as long as I have this," Brent patted his wooden staff.

"We'll see you tomorrow. The guys are starting to get antsy."

Brent chuckled and watched as the two men went back to their container.

He parted the tent flap and bumped directly into Olron. "Were you listening?"

"Yes." Olron put both hands on Brent's arms. "I wanted to be sure you were safe."

"They're okay. I've been with vampires before."

Said Makrah from behind his curtain, "They're after one thing: power and blood."

"That's two things."

"Blood contains power." Makrah parted his curtain.

Brent couldn't see much beyond it. There was a light on back there — not an electric light because no electricity came into the tent.

"They take our blood, and with magic and spells, they can know us. If they know us, they can control us."

"Did you have a vampire control you?" asked Brent.

"Never," said Makrah, "And I will not start now." Makrah snapped shut the curtain.

Olron still had his hands on Brent's arms. He rubbed his hands up and down them. "C'mon, let's get you naked."

The next day dawned overcast again, and Brent left the TOC with Baldar's flight path. Baldar headed to the farthest west he could possibly go: Laghman Province. He was going to the Chekla village, on the banks of a river.

Kurt came with his handler, Billy. It was two weeks since the full moon, and Brent was surprised to see Kurt as a wolf for that long a period of time. He would have to ask Kurt why he remained as a wolf over the time of the full moon.

Dropped off two kilometers from Chekla, they walked south. It was late for them, past 0900, as they started walking into the village. They didn't expect Taliban here, so the men of JD Platoon (Whiskey on the official radio, but JD unofficially) were more relaxed. The village was bustling, people and animals walking through. The men gave the kids candy and trinkets while the sergeants with their translators looked for elders.

Brent hung back with Kurt and Billy. People stayed away from them, scared of the wolf at Billy's side. Billy had Kurt on a leash, though he didn't need one; it was more for the look than actual use.

The men milled around the village as the sergeant and his small entourage of three men followed a pair of men into a building. The men gathered closer to the building, to make sure it was safe. They stayed around the village until 1200, and there was no sign of Baldar.

At 1203, the sergeant and his men left the building. Brent stayed out of the way as the sergeant called the men over. Then, they all turned to look at Brent.

Brent looked around to make sure that no one was behind him, as the sergeant beckoned him over.

"I know you're a wizard," said the sergeant, SHOWTON, it said on his tunic, "But are you a dowser?"

"No, sir," said Brent, giving him the title out of respect for him and the fact that he was in charge of the platoon around him. "But I have a simple spell for purifying small amounts of water."

Sergeant Showton shook his head. "They need drinkable water and they're having a fight with the neighboring village for a spring."

"Sorry, sir, I can't help with that."

"Maybe if we build a water purifying plant?" said another man.

Brent backed his way out of the group and went to a building where he could see through the grimy windows of a school. Kids were in seats, a teacher writing something on a blackboard, and it all looked so normal to him. They weren't quite in the middle of a war zone, but this was one of the violent and remote areas. He stood watching the kids, and his mind wondered about Chrissie. *Would she want children?*

He blinked. *Where did that come from?*

"Hey, Wizard," called Billy.

The platoon had formed up and was heading out.

Still no Baldar. Brent followed the men as they walked past the village, out toward the mountains. Something nagged at him, saying this was a bad idea, but he thought that it was more a bad feeling that Baldar wasn't around.

The men had their hands on their guns. They were wary. Kurt's hackles were up as they walked into the shade of the mountain.

"You feel it too, huh?" said Billy, trying to soothe the wolf.

Brent sensed a bad, nasty feeling in his stomach, and held his staff across his body. It was already colder than the village, and there was snow at the top of the mountain.

"Sarge, we're not going mountain climbing, are we?"

"No," called Showton. "We're going to check out this cave Scott saw." They would blame Scott for what happened.

Scott, however, was not the lead, but a young freckle-faced, typical-looking farm boy with an itchy trigger finger. As he stepped out of an outcrop of rocks, he got shot. His body armor took the bullet, but he was still knocked off his feet.

Another man jumped forward and dragged Scott back to the outcrop of rocks. Ten men could not stay behind two three-foot tall piles of rock. There was only that one shot; no withering fire.

"Sniper," said Showton as the medic looked over Scott.

Brent stood by in case he was needed for a healing.

"Not a very good one," said the medic. "You're lucky. Got you right in the chest."

"Lucky? I feel like someone just ran me over."

"Better than having a hole in your heart, right?"

"Sir," said Billy, "I have sniper training."

Kurt whined.

Billy looked down at the wolf and smiled. "I'll be okay, bro."

"You got a rifle?" asked Showton.

"I can use my own rifle. It's not a sniper rifle, but it'll do the job."

"Go ahead," said Showton. "You need a spotter?"

Billy took out a scope from one of his bags. "No, sir."

Billy aimed the gun between a couple of rocks, up toward where the shot might have come from. Meanwhile Scott was moved to the rear, and Brent got out of the way. He noticed above them sat an outcropping of rock that he could easily explode, but then it would cause an avalanche and bury his own men. So that idea wasn't feasible.

As the men waited for Billy to set up, no other shots came from the area.

"I don't see him," said Billy, and stood up.

In a split second, Kurt tackled Billy, throwing him to the ground. An explosion of blood came from Kurt's haunch as he fell with a yelp of pain.

"Shit!" cried Billy.

Kurt whined again, this time in pain, and looked at his back leg. It had been almost blown off.

"I got this," said Brent, as he yanked Kurt off Billy.

Kurt almost snapped at him as Brent pulled him toward the rear. Brent held his hands over the gushing wound as Kurt lay his head down on the ground.

Brent knew he could heal the werewolf, provided that he was a born werewolf, not turned. Turned werewolves were more magical, and immune to his magic. One of the archmages at the academy offered the analogy that magic healing on a magical creature was like pouring fire on fire. It made things worse. Born werewolves were considered "mutations" and not magical at all.

Brent started the spell as he saw the red aura around the wound. "I don't know what to do," he told Kurt. "I'll stop the bleeding, but I can't rebuild it. I don't know wolf anatomy."

Kurt whined and seemed to nod. Brent found the artery supplying most of the blood. He found both ends and rebuilt the artery. A whoop went up from the men at one point, but Brent ignored it, as he continued with his work. Finally, he turned to the medic and saw that the members of the platoon stood up, looking out at the mountain.

"I need a brace for him," said Brent. "He's got no functioning muscles in his leg."

"I got him," said a burly Marine.

He picked up Kurt like he was a sack of rice, hoisting him around his shoulders. Kurt yelped in pain as he was manhandled.

"Take him back," said the medic.

"Wizard," said Showton, "You'd better go with him."

Brent nodded, and followed the Marine down the mountain to the village. Another platoon was there, and they called a helicopter to extract Kurt and Brent back to FOB Blessing.

Kurt lay in the back of the helicopter, his head on Brent's lap the entire way. Brent kept petting him, not knowing what else to do. If Kurt shifted to human, he could help him. But some werewolves didn't like to shift in public because they would end up being naked. Besides, there wasn't enough room for him to shift into a human, anyway, the chopper being laden with medical supplies.

At FOB Blessing, Kurt was taken into the hospital container. They lay him on a gurney and chased Brent out.

He went back to his tent to get his kit off and bumped into Baldar.

"Hey," he said.

"Hey?" said Baldar. "What a strange word."

"It's a sound of greeting."

"I know what it is," said Baldar. "I have been around you humans for too long."

"What do you have against us?"

"It is not all humans. Just you."

"I told you that I'm not in this to control you."

"You control Tyrath."

"What? How?"

"He does what you tell him now. He has no rider."

"He chose that himself." Brent went into the dim tent. "Jesus, don't you guys talk to each other?"

"I dislike the fire dragons. Tyrath is too angry; Olron is too happy."

"You need to compromise. What about the guys you play games with?"

"What about them?"

Brent pulled off his belts one by one, while Baldar stood in the doorway. "You could be friends with them."

"I do not want to be friends with humans."

"You have to trust sometime, Baldar."

"I live alone. I do not need friends."

"Friends help each other. Like I'm helping you."

Baldar crossed his arms. "How?"

"How else would you get to eat?"

"You do that to satisfy Makrah."

"I do that to satisfy all of you."

"Because if you do not, Tyrath and Olron will hunt."

"What about you? Don't you hunt?"

"Not here. In the mountains, I may."

"You like penguins and polar bears over goats and sheep?"

"I do not know of any polar bears where I live."

Brent sighed. "Tough room," he muttered, taking off the last belt.

He glanced at his watch: he had missed the auction for the day, which meant he had to go to Gimblr to get the animals.

"Excuse me, I have to go pick up your dinner."

"I will wait," said Baldar. He followed Brent outside.

The *whoomp* of mortars woke Brent out of a sound sleep. Olron sat up immediately. "That was too close," he said.

Tyrath came out of his area. "I will take care of this," he said, storming out to the entrance.

Brent started to follow, but Olron put a hand on his arm. "No."

Brent shook off Olron's hand and went to the front of the tent. Tyrath stood there, looking up at the mountains. Brent came up behind him, Olron following.

Another mortar came in, close enough to rock the ground for them to feel it beneath their bare feet.

"I will take care of this," said Tyrath again, glaring up at the mountain.

Brent said, "You don't have any orders —"

Tyrath whirled on Brent. "To the devil with your orders! They are attacking us."

Brent stepped back, bumping into Olron. Makrah and Baldar both came out of the tent. Tyrath jogged a few yards ahead.

"Close your eyes," said Olron to Brent, "or you'll be blinded."

Brent did it reluctantly. He wanted to see how the dragons shifted, but in this case, maybe it was better to follow Olron's advice. He saw a flash beyond his lids, like when the sun bathed a person's closed eyes.

When he opened his eyes again, black smoke wafted directly in front of him. Through the smoke, he could see the red lizard-like dragon, wings outstretched and ready for flight.

Brent realized that he wouldn't be able to see much in the dark, so he turned and went back into the tent for his NVG's. The dragons could see just fine in the dark.

Olron followed again. "Brent —"

"They might have been baiting you to come out," said Brent, digging out the NVG's.

Another mortar hit, closer this time. No one seemed to be returning fire.

"Tyrath knows what he's doing," said Olron.

With the NVG's on, Olron was bathed in dark green. He could easily see things in the tent.

"He trusts you, so you should trust him."

"Why do you say that?"

"He shifted in front of you. Either he trusts you or wanted to blind you for life. Let's assume the former?"

Brent looked to the side section of the tent. Makrah had left his curtain open. Brent could see an old-fashioned pirate chest, darker green than what was spilling out of it. They looked like bright green coins. Olron put his arm around Brent's to drag him away. Brent let himself get pulled to the tent's entrance.

Tyrath flew to the mountain at their east. He could see Tyrath as a darker green shadow in the green background of stars and night.

The dragon hovered over a small group of leafless trees. Brent thought he could see movement, like ants running out of an anthill. A huge burst of flame came out of the dark green shadow — a bright green jet. The trees turned into smoldering matchsticks; the fire didn't spread because there was nothing around it but rocks.

Tyrath followed the ants, picking them off one by one, small bursts of flame on the ground that went out moments later. Tyrath turned south, to the other mountainside that faced closer to the base itself.

Brent couldn't see the ants, but knew that Tyrath took his time, burning outcrops of trees and exploding piles of rocks. Then Tyrath winged his way back.

Although he looked ungainly, he landed with grace and stared at Brent. He opened his mouth to show the wicked rows of teeth and spat out a gout of flame that landed a couple of feet away from where Brent stood. It messed up his NVG readings.

Then, in the next second, Olron jumped in front of Brent. Brent flinched, closing his eyes, but saw the flash behind the lids. He pulled back when the flash ended.

As the black smoke wafted away, could perceive Tyrath before him, his long hair cascading down his bare chest.

Brent swallowed, staring at the naked Tyrath for a long moment. Tyrath stared back, his red eyes glowing.

"They will not be bothering us anymore," he said, and went back into the tent.

Brent doubted that.

A couple of days later, the vampires found Brent at the dragons' tent. Jack looked fine, but Jamie looked a little worse for wear.

"Haven't fed?" asked Brent of Jamie.

"I'll be fine." However, he watched a man walking by as if he was meat.

Jack said, "We're as tough as Marines when we have to be."

Brent asked, "Nobody registered?"

"I said I'll be fine."

Jack shook his head. "It doesn't have to do with the registration. He's got a type."

"I do not," said Jamie.

"Then why do you prefer the big guys?"

"Because their blood is stronger."

"I'm going to the gym," said Brent.

Jamie brightened. *Was Jamie gay?* he wondered. But he had no right to ask, and even if Jamie admitted it, he couldn't help, since he wasn't a big, strong Marine.

"Maybe you'll find someone there," said Jack.

"Doubt it," said Jamie, but he went anyway.

The three men walked into the gym. All of the weight benches had been taken up by burly Marines and some other men that Brent didn't know. He could tell by their tattoos that they were Navy guys. Jack and Jamie nodded to them, while Brent waited at the side for an available bench.

He noticed two men — one Sailor, one Marine — straining. They were trying to outdo each other. Finally, the Sailor placed the weight on the rack and sat up.

"That all?" said the Marine, placing his weight on his rack.

"I can do a hell of a lot more, but I didn't know if you could count that high."

Barbells dropped from all over the place with a loud *clang* as men stood up. Jack put a hand on Brent's shoulder. He didn't know if that meant he was not to get involved or if it meant he was not to be fucked with. Brent thought it was he wouldn't get involved, and he hung back, stepping away from the two men who got in each other's faces.

"You sayin' I'm stupid?"

"I'm sayin' that you might not be ready for a job more complicated than handing out lollipops to kids."

"At least we don't blow shit up by mistake."

"I never blew up anything by mistake."

"Or on fucking purpose."

The two men glared at each other. Marines outnumbered the Navy team.

Jack let go of Brent and stepped forward. "Howe, enough."

Jamie stayed in the back, watching the two men almost bumping chests. Brent did not risk getting near Jamie. Obviously these two were his "type".

Howe turned as if suddenly seeing Jack for the first time. In fact, they all looked at him, Marines and Navy alike, with looks ranging from anger to disgust to confusion. Howe stepped away from the Marine. He reached down on the weight bench and picked up his own shirt. With one final glare at Jack, he stormed out, Jamie hot on his heels.

The Navy guys got their things together and left. Brent thought it best to leave as well, since Jack put a hand on Brent's shoulder to guide him to the door. He didn't know if the Marines would let him back in the weight room after the vampires left.

"I think we've worn out our welcome," Jack said as the stood together in front of the building. "We'll probably leave soon. I'll ask for orders."

Brent only nodded.

"I'd better go check on Jamie. You'll be all right?"

"There's enough men on base that I can yell if someone comes after me."

Jack patted Brent's shoulder and went out into the barracks. Brent cautiously walked back to the dragons' tent.

The next afternoon, Tyrath went off the grid again. The lieutenant colonel was there at the time and whirled on Brent.

"Rogers! You and Dog Company find that bastard."

Brent went to Dog Company's tent and told them of their orders. They had just come back that morning, so were none too happy to be going out again on less than four hours' sleep.

Dog Company was headed up by a huge Marine named Big Fur, a nickname from his real name, Fiebig. A hairy brute of a man who had five o'clock shadow by noon, he was able to summon up a platoon and get them kitted out while Brent got his own kit, his staff, and the flight path of the dragon.

At least the alleged flight path, Brent hoped.

If Tyrath stayed on course, heading to the Kunar province in the Korangal Valley, he would head toward another Forward Operating Base, Salerno. FOB Salerno and its surrounding Fire Bases hadn't seen him.

Brent went in the lead vehicle, sensing out for IED's, while someone else read the map to the driver. Brent had them stop a few times, once between a mountain range and a poppy field. Brent got out of the vehicle. He felt something at first, like a wall against his magic.

The men dismounted, looking around. "What's wrong?" one asked.

"There's something out there," Brent said, "But I can't figure out what it is." He tried to give a push against the "wall" that he sensed.

A breeze blew by, carrying with it a deep, earthy scent. As he scrunched his face in confusion, a wave of force hit him directly in the solar plexus. He doubled over, and a triumphant yell came from the direction of the mountainside in front of him. All the Marines readied their guns.

Then horses and men burst out through the brush. The Marines didn't think about it; they fired.

Brent caught his breath as Big Fur yanked him to the Humvee and shoved him against it.

"Get down!"

Brent dove to the dirt. A Marine ran past him, shooting at the horses. He heard animals and men scream as they fell under the hail of bullets. Brent turned his head to see a man clad in white from turban to feet, brandishing an Arabic scimitar, heading toward him.

His staff, dropped when he got hit, lay a couple of feet away. He focused on it to try and pull it to him with his magic. Meanwhile, the man in white was being peppered with bullets, no blood on his clothes, only black, smoking holes. He did not stop.

Brent's staff flew to his hand while the man in white toppled off his horse as it fell. Yet still the man got up.

"What the fuck!" yelled a Marine and unloaded his AR into the man.

More smoking holes appeared in the white cloth, as the man walked like someone heading into a strong wind.

"Vampire!" yelled Brent, trying to scramble to his feet. "Sunlight kills them!"

Big Fur tackled the man, throwing him to the ground. He struggled with him as Brent finally got to his feet. He tried to think of a spell that would attack the vampire without hurting Big Fur or himself.

Big Fur ripped off the vampire's the turban and face coverings. The man screamed as he threw his gloved hands up to cover his face. He started to burn on his own accord, as Big Fur pulled strip after strip of cloth away from the man's body. The vampire turned to run in Brent's direction, who had the only shade in the immediate area. Big Fur pulled the vampire back, holding onto the back of the vampire's robes.

The vampire tugged himself forward, his face black and burnt, his hands reaching for Brent. The tunic tore out of Big Fur's fist, exposing the vampire's back to the sun.

The vampire gurgled as his skin turned black, smelling like burning flesh. He took two steps toward Brent, who turned to the side and held his staff like a bat. He swung, aiming low. The staff connected with the creature's torso and the staff's center exploded in blue light and shards of wood. The head of the staff went flying, while Brent held onto a half meter of the wood.

The vampire fell to his knees to look up at Brent. Brent turned the pointed edge of the staff he had in his hand and aimed it at the creature's chest. His flesh was mostly gone, and he was down to his bones and a black sack of something among his ribs. His face, a blackened skull, smoldered in the sunlight.

He fell forward. Brent walked up to his torso, holding the spiked part of the staff. He put it between a pair of ribs and thrust down. It pierced the black flesh in between, and a geyser of black blood burst from the creature, splashing Brent with it. The vampire erupted into dust.

The firefight ended while the vampire burned. When it was safe, the Marines gathered around the ashes. Brent kicked at them, mixing them with the dirt. He pulled out a small packet of white crystals and added that to the pile.

"Salt," he said to the Marines gathered around. "To make sure he never rises again. It's a purifier."

He found the head of his staff a few feet away. He picked up all three pieces and held them in his hands. He initially tried to fit them back together, but it was no use. It was dead. He didn't know if the Magic Corps would give him a new one. He had worked with this staff since Boot.

"Shit, man," said one of the men.

Brent frowned. "Yeah."

"Can you still do magic?" asked Big Fur.

"Not at a distance." He tossed the shards into the Humvee.

"Should we keep going?"

Brent looked up at the sky. "Do you want to get caught in these mountains at night?"

"Wouldn't be the first time."

"Tyrath might be coming back soon enough. Depends on if he found something to burn."

"You don't think he's not following the flight path?"

"I *know* he's not."

"We should get some higher ground if we're gonna be sleeping in the trucks."

Big Fur said, "If we go to base, we get back out three hours later. We might as well keep going to get some shut eye. "Where's the flight path again?"

Brent pulled out the map. Big Fur got his binoculars and looked out at the mountain. "We can make the summit by nightfall."

"Provided we don't get ambushed," said Brent.

"Especially by vampires."

They piled back into the Humvees and headed out.

After a couple of stops, they arrived at the low summit of one of the smaller mountains. Wide enough for three Humvees to circle round, the men gathered for cold rations and took shifts guarding while others slept. Brent drew the dawn shift.

He dreamed fitfully, seeing Scar as the vampire coming at him. He never got to see the vampire's face. But he knew Scar wasn't a vampire.

"Sir?" he heard someone call him in his dream.

He snapped open his eyes, tried to focus in the dark. A man had his hand on his shoulder, shaking him.

"Sir? Someone outside to see you."

"Someone out — what?"

"That's what I said, sir."

Brent unfolded himself out of the cramped seat of the Humvee and climbed out of the truck. In the starlight and the half-moon, he followed the Marine to the center of the three trucks.

"Magus," said Olron, coming up to him. Olron wore only a pair of shorts. Brent didn't kiss him, caress him, or even touch him. Brent felt the blood rush to his face. "We were worried."

"I-I'm sorry, I forgot all about getting goats before I left —"

"I don't care about that." He finally did reach out and gripped Brent's forearm. "I was worried."

The Marine who came to get him walked away. Brent couldn't assume he was alone with Olron, so he showed no displays of affection. "I'm okay," he said.

"I'm staying here," Olron studied him. "I'll escort you all home tomorrow."

"Is Tyrath back at the base?"

"Yes, he was there when I left."

"Shit." Brent took that opportunity to step away from Olron. "I knew that was going to happen."

"Why did you come all the way out here?"

"We were looking for Tyrath. He went off the grid again."

"He hunts. It's what he does."

"You're a red dragon. How come you don't hunt?"

He shrugged. "It might have to do with him being a Russian dragon."

Brent looked around. "I don't think there's anywhere for you to sleep, Olron."

"Who said anything about sleep?" Olron stuck his hands in the pockets of his shorts. Brent knew from experience that there was nothing on underneath.

"I can't stay up all night."

"Sleep if you need to, then. I'll guard this area."

"By yourself?"

"By myself." Olron backed away from Brent. "I'll be here." Then he ducked between two of the Humvees and disappeared into the woods.

Brent looked around him, but if the Marine guards were awake, they didn't seem to be anywhere that he could see. He heard a crash in the direction Olron had gone. As he started to walk that way, he saw the big red dragon come out of the woods. Tall and majestic, Olron raised his head, silhouetted against the half-moon for a moment. He brought his head down to Brent's level. His head was thinner than Tyrath's, an elongated snout. He gently pushed his head into Brent's side, almost toppling him over. A low growl echoed in the dark.

Brent put his hand on Olron's head, careful of the nostrils and the teeth. Olron turned from him, and Brent could see that Olron carried something in one of his claws.

A pair of camo shorts.

It took a full day to get back. The lieutenant from the TOC decided never to send Brent or anyone after Tyrath again. Brent, exhausted from lack of comfortable sleep, cradled the three parts of his staff while he headed to the dragons' tent when someone tapped him on the shoulder.

"Jesus Christ," Brent said, jumping back from Jack appearing behind him. "You scared the shit out of me."

"Habit," said Jack. He was clad head to toe in black because the sun was out. "We got our new orders. We're shipping out tonight."

Brent had lost his staff, and now he was going to lose his protection, too. Unless, of course, Olron would step in.

"You gonna be okay?" asked Jack.

"Yeah. Yeah, I'll be okay." The vampire that came after him ... wait. Was it.?

It bounced magic off him, hitting Brent in the gut. His magic didn't kill the vampire — the stake did. Brent thought that the vampire had something against magic. Was the vampire a Black Lion? It didn't stop until Brent killed it —

"You okay?" Jack asked again.

"Yeah, yeah. Thinking."

"Sorry. Good luck."

"Yeah." The Black Lions were vampires? Or were some vampires Black Lions?

Brent walked slowly to the dragons' tent. He carried the three bits of wood as if they were relics, like remnants of his favorite clothes. He didn't know what to do with them. Did they have magic in them? The center piece was still soaked with the vampire's black blood.

At the tent, Baldar came out. "Magus," he said in greeting.

"Baldar."

Baldar motioned at the wood in Brent's hand. "What is that?"

"My staff. I broke it."

Baldar showed no emotion as he said, "I did not think that possible. What are you going to do with it?"

"I don't know." He figured at worst he could put them in this bag and send an email to the Archmage to find out what to do. Maybe he had to burn them to get rid of his magical essence. "Where are you headed?"

"To try tacos."

"Shit, the goats." It was too late to go to Gimblr now.

Baldar said, "You worry too much about that."

"Makrah said —"

"Makrah is old and used to servants to bring him food." Baldar came closer. "He is a rich man in Budapest and must carry his riches whereever he goes."

"Oh, really?" That must be the open chest he saw the night when Tyrath attacked the mortars.

"Truly," said Baldar. "Why do you think he prefers to stay here all the time?"

12

KUNAR PROVINCE AND ASLAMABAD

A COUPLE OF DAYS LATER, Brent approached the TOC. The lieutenant colonel wasn't there and no one asked about Tyrath anymore.

In the Tactical Operational Command, as the men watched the drones, and the drones watched the people outside villages. Afghans worked in the fields in the early morning hours before the sun got too high in the sky. Brent sat on the side, away from the specialists. Cooler in the TOC than it was outside, Brent found himself dozing.

"Cinder Two —"

Brent jerked awake. The tone of voice sounded concerned.

Cinder Two is Olron, he thought.

"Cinder Two is down," said the radio man. "Repeat, Cinder Two is down."

"Is he supposed to be?"

"He was taking heavy fire —"

Brent jumped up. "Down? Where?"

The radio man was already going to the map. "Here —" he pointed to a microscopic village. "South of Nevek."

Brent said, turning to the lieutenant in charge of the TOC, "I need a ride there."

The lieutenant glared at the map. "You'll have to take a bird. It's hundreds of kilometers away."

Brent couldn't get a helicopter. He wasn't that high ranking.

"Where's Makrah? Baldar?" He knew better than to ask about Tyrath, who was probably off the grid again.

"Frostfire is engaged here." The commander pointed to a spot in the mountains. "Icelander is —"

Said another voice, "Icelander is on patrol with support —"

"I'll need him," said Brent, heading to the door.

The commander said, "But —"

"I said I need him!"

Brent ran out the door, dashing back out to the landing area where the dragons took off in the morning. It took forever.

Where was Olron? Did they find him? Was he injured? And what am I going to do when I get there?

He saw Baldar from a distance, sunlight glinting off his armor, winging his way toward him. Brent realized he didn't have a parachute, so if he fell, he wouldn't have long to utter the flying spell.

Baldar landed gracefully. He bent forward. Brent tore out the radio from the saddle and the makeshift headphones from Baldar's ear.

"We need to go to Nevek! Olron's down!"

Brent climbed up into the saddle and held onto the pommel. Baldar leapt into the air. Brent thought he left his stomach behind.

The air rushed into his face as the dragon flew, his wings producing a *whomp-whomp* sound as they propelled him through the air. Brent buried his face against Baldar's scaly neck.

Brent felt Baldar roar — a mighty angry bellow — as he turned in the air. He seemed to be homing in on something, heading into the Pesh valley at high speed. Brent glanced up to see them coming upon a village that looked slightly bigger than it had on the map. They flew low over it, drawing fire. Baldar roared and cast his head about. Brent felt bullets cut the air next to him and hunkered down in the saddle. He almost lay on top of it.

They heard a scream of agony. Not a human scream, but of an animal trapped, dying. Baldar swooped around. Brent could see below them a black elongated spot that, as they got closer, resolved itself to be Olron in dragon form in a pool of black blood. Olron raised his head and cried out in pain.

Baldar landed close to Olron. Brent fell off the saddle, landing hard on his side. He struggled up, ignoring the pain, assessing Olron.

Thick, black blood pooled beneath the dragon from a gash almost as big as a HumVee in his belly. Brent walked through the muck and touched Olron's chest.

Brent didn't know what to do. He closed his eyes and concentrated, wondering if dragon physiology was the same as men's. Baldar had Olron's head cradled in his claws. Orlon moaned.

If I send healing energy, Brent thought, *maybe he can help himself.* Brent thought the spell and let it go.

Olron screamed, arching his back, and the wound gushed black blood into the sand. Olron lay his head against Baldar. He didn't move. He didn't breathe.

Baldar slowly set Olron's head down onto the ground.

I killed him, Brent thought, removing his hands, covered in sticky, black blood that smelled like sulfur. His eyes welled up.

Baldar roared, agony and grief filling the air.

A loud thump sounded from behind Brent. Tyrath had landed and walked up to Olron. Makrah arrived soon after, landing behind Olron's body. Olron's body and blood became luminescent. Brent bolted away — his hands and boots were also luminescent. In a moment of bright light, like a sun, Olron's body became encased in fire. Brent's hands were not on fire, nor were his boots, but the blood on them had disappeared.

Baldar stepped out of the fire. Tyrath roared in rage, launching into the air, kicking up dust. Makrah took off after him.

Tyrath headed to the village, flying very low. Makrah came up behind him and wrapped him with his tail. Tyrath beat his wings to get away, but Makrah was both bigger and stronger.

Meanwhile, the flames in the desert died down, leaving the sand with chunks of red glass. Brent saw something white in the mess. He walked in the hot sand, ignoring the battling dragons, avoiding the hot, molten glass.

He heard a screech and looked up to see the dragons locked in an embrace, tumbling to the ground. They landed hard in the north side of the village, crashing into houses.

Brent gazed at the white object. It was a bone, flat and about as long as his forearm, with rounded edges. He picked it up — it was warm to the touch, and had symbols etched on it.

Brent was not about to get in the middle of the dragons' catfight. Baldar looked like he didn't want to, either, as he sat with his wings and head bent. People evacuated the village, running toward him. The dragons roared and flew a few feet above the houses, then crashed down again. This time only one dragon rose.

Makrah looked a lot worse for wear, bleeding shimmering blue liquid, struggling hard to keep aloft. He flew down to the spot Olron had been. The two dragons, remaining as dragons, sat in stony silence, staring at the molten sand with Brent.

"Cinder Two flew within RPG range," said Brent calmly. "It's unknown if he was hit by us or them."

Brent had already done his crying with Makrah and Baldar. When the ANA came upon them, Brent was dry-eyed and pissed-off. He took it on himself to investigate.

"We don't fire RPG's if there's air support," said Lieutenant Colonel Schiffer.

Brent reported his findings to Schiffer's office in HQ. "Regardless of what Lieutenant Waters might have believed, sir, the dragons are not indestructible or immortal. They die, especially against mortars and RPG's."

The lieutenant colonel tapped his lips with his fingertips. "What about the other three dragons?"

"Makrah put Tyrath in his place while they destroyed the village. Baldar hasn't left the tent."

"They need to get back out there."

"Sir," said Brent, "They're all volunteers."

"They come under our rules."

"Sir. They will walk away." He let that sink in before continuing. "They're not mobile cavalry or armored tanks. They're intelligent creatures, with their own minds and ideas. They're natives and we need to treat them like that."

"Or what? They'll turn on us?"

He didn't think Makrah would let them do that. But just in case, Brent had to bring it up. "Sir, our planes versus dragons?"

Brent could see Schiffer visualizing it. He shook his head. "I want to know if they're staying or going. Find out."

As Brent headed to the dragons' tent, he stopped to see Jen and Deb. Meghan told them what happened. Deb was especially broken up, but she was a Marine, and didn't let Brent see her tears.

Brent still carried the bone in the left inside pocket of his shirt. He patted his shirt as he headed to the dragons' tent in the dimming light of the day.

Makrah sat outside, not smoking for once. He glared angrily at Brent. "We have no food."

"Is that all you fucking care about!" Brent gave the same look back at Makrah. "All you care about is yourself and your fucking stomach. One of your own died today."

"He has no need of food or your tears."

Brent took the two steps that separated them. He cocked his arm back to punch Makrah, who stood with a flat look on his face. When Brent swung, Makrah held up his hand and easily caught the punch. Brent struggled to pull his arm back, but Makrah was stronger, holding him.

"You can bring him back someday," said Makrah calmly. "You are a magus."

Makrah brought his arm down and released Brent's hand. Brent took in a breath, feeling the heat of the bone against his ribs.

Brent summoned a dim blue mage light. He looked up at the four curtained areas of the tent, knowing which one was Olron's. He parted the curtain to Olron's room, sending the mage light into the area.

All around Olron's cot were shelves made from plywood and pallets, stacked precariously one on top of another, five "bookcases" with six very thin shelves each. He sent the mage light deeper into the area to illuminate it in a dull blue glow.

Brent stepped inside and looked at one of the thin shelves. The thickness of a pallet, it was too thin to hold books. He peered in, to see all sorts of tiny metal cars in different condition. Some were perfect; some rusted and old.

"'Matchboxes' he called them," said Tyrath.

Brent jerked his head up. "Tyrath! I'm sorry, I never looked in your section —"

"I would have known if you did." He stepped inside, looking around. "This must all be destroyed now."

"Why?"

"Who would want them?"

"The soldiers can give them to the kids."

Tyrath said, "I will ask Makrah." He turned to leave.

"Tyrath, I'm sorry."

"Why? It is not your fault."

He took a shuddering breath. He looked at the area where his cot was, then back at Tyrath.

The curtain at Tyrath's area slammed shut, leaving Brent in the dim light. Even that disappeared, his concentration gone.

He sat on the cot inside Olron's area. He looked around the room, at the different Matchboxes. He heard someone come into the tent.

Baldar peered into the room. He focused momentarily on Brent, then stepped into the area. Brent wanted to have the room by himself.

"I am leaving," said Baldar.

"What?"

"I will die if I remain. I miss my home." He turned to leave.

"Wait!"

Brent got off the cot and stood next to Baldar, who was just as powerfully built as the other dragons, but blue and without definition. Baldar stared unblinkingly at Brent. But he had nothing to say.

Finally, after a couple of uncomfortable minutes that seemed far too long, Baldar turned away and left.

★ ★ ★

Chrissie —

A good friend has died under my care. I couldn't save him.
He got too close to an RPG. He got shot down. I tried to save
him, but

Brent crumpled up the letter. He needed to tell someone what happened. He wasn't sure if the chaplain would understand.

The tent felt stuffy all of a sudden. He left his area and went outside in the pre-dawn hours. The dragons had no orders now that they were down to two members. Brent knew he would have to go to the TOC later to find out what to do next.

Of course, because there were only two dragons left, there may not be a Marine Fifth Wing anymore. It depended on Captain Laurence and what he decided. Brent supposed he should be on that conference call when it happens. It also depended on whether Makrah or Tyrath would want to continue.

He walked over to the helos to see the men load up the Ospreys for the morning's patrol. One man looked his way and walked slowly with a slight limp toward to him. Thinking that he was going to get told to leave, he started to turn away.

"Hey, Wizard."

Brent turned at the voice to see a brown-haired Marine. "Kurt?"

"Yah." He stopped in front of Brent.

"How's your leg?"

Kurt stretched out his leg and flexed it. "Not too bad. Healed mostly on its own, but if you hadn't put it together, I might've lost it." He stood straight. "I want to thank you."

"I tried my best."

Kurt tilted his head. "You okay, man?"

"We lost a dragon yesterday. He got shot down."

"Shit, I'm sorry." Kurt put a hand on Brent's shoulder.

"Thanks."

"Were you close?"

His "yeah" came out more strangled than he wanted to.

Kurt said, "I've been there."

Brent nodded.

"The full moon's in a few days. We will mourn for him."

Brent swallowed. "Thanks. I appreciate it."

"We are all Children of the Moon, Wizard. Even you, by extension."

Brent went back to the tent. He thought about what Makrah said, that he could bring Olron back. He was too exhausted to even summon a mage light as he went back to his cot. He lay down, staring up at the ceiling of the tent.

He figured he had passed out, because when he woke up, it was still dark. He sat up on the edge of the cot, rubbing his eyes.

He heard someone pull back a curtain. He peered into the aisle that his cot faced, trying to see who it was.

"You are awake," said Makrah.

Brent didn't want to talk to him. He still wanted to punch him.

"What will happen to us?"

"I don't know," Brent said. "I have to go to the TOC and see what's going on." Brent stood up and stretched. "You have the day off, I guess." He pulled on his tunic. When he got it over his head and looked back at the aisle, Makrah was gone.

After scrounging up some breakfast at mess, he carried his coffee to the TOC, which had already been awake and at work for at least three hours. Brent stepped inside and Lieutenant Cruz nodded to him. Cruz was in charge of the TOC when the other commanders had days off.

Brent saluted. "Sorry about your dragon," said Cruz quietly.

"We've lost two of them."

"Two?" Cruz leaned back.

"Baldar left last night."

Cruz muttered, "Aw, fuck."

"I think we'd better call a meeting."

"Yeah," said Cruz. He glanced around the TOC. "Nothing special going on today. Baxter. Lupe. Go tell Lieutenant Colonel Schiffer and Lieutenant Briggs that we need a meeting pronto."

An hour later, in the conference room off from the TOC, Brent stood up in front of the group and told them all about Baldar's leaving.

"I tried talking him into staying," said Brent, "But he was adamant."

"Great," said Schiffer. "Makrah and Tyrath already don't sound like they like sticking around."

"Makrah is honorable," said Brent. "Tyrath will do what Makrah tells him, I think."

"You think?"

"I don't know. He knows we need him more than he needs us."

Schiffer crossed his arms and looked pissed. The rest of the higher ups also didn't look happy.

"At least the elections are coming up," said one of the lieutenants.

"That doesn't help things here. Did you tell Captain Laurence?"

Brent said, "Not yet, sir."

"Get him on the horn."

They were able to conference-call him in, and Brent again told how Olron died and Baldar left.

After Laurence went into a tirade of how the dragons couldn't just walk off whenever the hell they felt like it, Brent heard him say, "Besides, CTF Thunder is going to be disbanded in time for the elections anyway."

The men looked at each other across the table. Schiffer still sat, impassive, his arms crossed.

"So does that mean the Fifth Wing is going to be disbanded?" asked Brent.

"They're going to Kabul. Might as well do it now."

Brent found himself rocking away from the speakerphone. The men sat in stony silence.

"Get them packed up and moved out for Kabul," said Laurence. "I'll get the orders started." He hung up.

Everyone looked at Schiffer.

"You heard the man."

"You look horrible."

Brent half-smiled at Meghan. "Thanks."

"Want to sit down?" She took a step back into the container, to let him by if he wanted to go into the barracks.

"Actually, I want to know if Jen's around."

"She's at work. What do you need?"

"Her computer."

"You can use mine."

Brent followed her into the barracks. Nobody else was in the room, and it was cool even without the air conditioning running. She opened the chair to a desk she had cobbled together with plywood and sawhorses. Brent sat down and placed the heavy tome he carried next to the computer.

"What's that?"

"My grimoire."

"Your *what*?"

"Spell book."

He turned the heavy pages over to the last page, where he had drawn the symbols on Olron's bone. He searched on the Internet: first for Enochian, then for hieroglyphics. Neither matched.

"Dammit," he whispered, sitting back.

"What?" asked Meghan, looking up from a book.

"I found a relic and I don't know what these symbols mean." He showed them to her.

She got up from the cot and looked at his book. "Looks like Greek to me."

"It's not Greek. I wonder if it's Aramaic."

He tried that. He tried Hebrew, Russian...He surfed for three hours, and for his pain he found one symbol was for "Vesta", the Greek goddess of the hearth.

"This is hopeless," he said, slamming shut the book.

Meghan yawned.

"Sorry. I didn't mean to take up that much of your time."

She shrugged. "I wasn't going to do anything anyway."

Brent gathered his book. "I'll talk to some people. Maybe the Archmage knows. Thanks for letting me use the laptop."

"Anytime you want, sir."

He stepped out of the container. He heard a howl on the wind, one single lonely wolf. Then another joined it, mournful. Close by came another howl. Then another. It became a chorus, a pack of wolves all howling, not at the moon, because it was only at three-quarters, but for a Child of the Moon's death. Brent got chills while he stood listening.

Then it stopped, and one howl cried in the evening air.

13

ARCHMAGE DEITER STOOD in his purple robes, etching runes on the Humvees, when Brent and the dragons found him. Brent waited until he finished the sequence before stepping forward and saluting.

"First Magus," said Deiter, returning the salute. "Where's your staff?"

"I need a new one," said Brent. "Long story."

He looked past Brent to the dragons. "We were expecting you a lot earlier."

"We had to take care of a few things," Brent said.

The dragons had to pack. Baldar left with his GI Joes, leaving Makrah and Tyrath with their collections, packed in hard plastic totes. Brent packed some of the more precious-looking Matchboxes in a postal box and gave the rest to Dog Company to pass out to kids. They then had to wait for an Osprey to take them to Kabul, and, by the time they arrived, the day was mostly gone.

"You're stuck with whatever's left to camp out," said Deiter. "The Nighthawks already took your spot."

Brent had talked the dragons into at least putting shirts on, which they did, though they still were barefoot.

"I thought there were four of you."

"One of our number died in combat," said Makrah. "Another left before we were summoned here."

Deiter frowned. "This puts a dent in our plans."

The dragons shrugged, not caring.

"Come to my office. We'll discuss things there."

The three men followed Deiter to the Magic Corps HQ. The dragons looked up at the sign over the door. They hesitated.

"You'll be safe," said Brent.

Makrah went first. Tyrath followed.

"You're aware that most of the Corps are now in Iraq," said the archmage, sitting down at his bare desk.

"I understand that."

Brent allowed the dragons to sit, but they weren't budging from just inside the door. They both looked like they wanted to bolt out the door.

The archmage looked up at the dragons. "Come inside. I won't do anything."

"I will stay here," said Tyrath.

Makrah said, "What are our orders?"

"You will be a show of force during the elections. Fly around Kabul and look menacing."

"No riders? No radios?" asked Tyrath.

"No destroying things?" asked Makrah.

"No, no, and no."

If dragons could look disgusted, they did. Tyrath leaned against the doorframe, crossing his arms. The door suddenly opened, and Brent turned around.

Lieutenant Waters, clean-shaven, and in the purple robes of a magus, stood on the other side of the doorway. He stepped inside.

The dragons looked at the robes and stepped back.

"Starforce," said Dieter. "I believe you've met First Magus Rogers."

Brent wondered how Waters rated a codename.

"Oh, we've met," said Waters. He turned his attention to the dragons, "How are you guys doing? Where's Olron and Baldar?"

"Olron died in combat. Baldar returned home," said Makrah.

Waters said, looking at the archmage, "At least when I was liaison, nobody died."

"Not intentionally," said Brent.

"Enough." Deiter got their attention with that one word. Then he looked up at the dragons and smiled. "Would you excuse us?"

The dragons didn't move.

Brent said, "He wants to speak to us alone."

"Ah," said Makrah, and squeezed by Waters.

He snapped something Russian at Tyrath, who stood away from the wall and walked by Waters, closing the door quietly.

Dieter stood up. "If there's one thing that you're going to both learn, that's to work together. There are a total of twenty magi in the field — eleven from the last class, our largest class to date. Out of your class, Rogers, there's two. Yours, Starforce, four. Then there are the founders and the teachers." Dieter looked at each one of them. "You will work together so long as you're in the Magic Corps, is that understood?"

"Yes, sir," both men said, though they didn't sound enthusiastic.

"Now. Tomorrow, Rogers, you're going to a checkpoint and help out there. Starforce, you will continue to work on the trucks and trailers and place protection runes on them. Are there any questions?"

"No, sir," both men said.

"Send the dragons back in on your way out."

The two men saluted and left the room.

Brent held the door open for the dragons. "He wants to see you two."

Waters walked right by the dragons, heading to the main door. They'd have to work together, but that didn't mean they had to be friends.

Brent waited outside, just past the Magic Corps office. After some time, he saw the door open. The dragons and the archmage came out together. The dragons didn't look happy, but the archmage was talking to them. Brent couldn't hear what they were saying.

They walked together to a Humvee. The archmage got in the front, the two dragons in back, and they took off.

"Fine," Brent said to himself.

He looked for somewhere to bunk, finding the barracks at the far end of the camp. Some men smoking cigarettes outside nodded to him. Inside. a few video games were going on, and the noise level was pretty high. Brent wound his way through, asking if bunks were taken, finally finding one. The bunk next to that wasn't taken for obvious reasons, either — it was directly under a vent to outside, which meant it would be oppressively hot and constantly noisy.

Brent had been in much worse conditions, having slept in too many trucks to count, so this was perfectly fine for him. His bunkmate on the other side had a computer and was concentrating on something there. Brent started to unload.

He lay down, and the world fell away, the noise in the background fading to distant noise in his dreams, until someone shook him awake.

"Wizard," said a quiet voice.

Brent came out of sleep instantly. "Makrah?" He looked around; the barracks was quiet, hardly anyone inside.

"Yes." Tyrath, scowling, stood behind Makrah.

Brent sat up, rubbing sleep from his eyes. "What time is it?"

"1730," said Makrah, giving him room to get up.

Brent nodded to Tyrath, "What's wrong?"

"I do not like where we are staying."

Said Makrah, "We are where the Archmage placed us, close to him. Tyrath does not trust him."

I don't either, thought Brent. "Where did you go earlier?"

"A place that serves meat. We told your archmage that after the elections, we will not return."

Tyrath glared at Makrah. "He promised we would help during the elections,"

"What brought this about? Olron's death?"

"That," said Makrah, "and what he has said to us. How he treats us."

Uh oh, Brent thought.

"He believes we are armored machines."

"There are more of us in Iraq," said Tyrath. "More creatures that fly; creatures of myth and story."

"Basilisks and centaurs," said Makrah. "And other dragons."

"They are being used as what you call 'cannon fodder.' He said they are a 'high turnover.'"

Brent narrowed his eyes. Was the Army creating these creatures, or were they being found and discovered? "This is the first I've heard of it."

"We will not be used as cannon fodder," said Makrah.

"No, no, I don't blame you. How did the Archmage take that?"

"He was not happy, but said we were free to do what we wished."

"We are sleeping with the enemy," said Tyrath. "In his tent."

"The archmage isn't an enemy, Tyrath."

"He is no friend."

"Look, I'll try and talk to him tomorrow, okay? In the meantime, I'm sure you have some orders for tomorrow?"

The two dragons looked at each other. Tyrath shrugged.

"We will let you rest," said Makrah.

His orders were simple: There were no female ANPs. At this checkpoint, deep in Kabul, Brent was supposed to use his IED searching abilities to sweep the women and cars for bombs. Brent knew that the ancient Afghan culture would not allow men near women.

The name on the field lieutenant's uniform said Ledbetter, and he was older than Brent by a good five years or more.

"Magus, huh?" he said with a Midwest accent.

"You'll see," said Brent.

Brent went to the ANP and the three uniformed Army men and introduced himself. If he used his normal "Raise the Enemy" spell, a good 90% of the people there would be flying. Instead, he had to go by his gut, which he wasn't sure was accurate.

Most of the time, the ANP deferred to him. He stood in front of cars, his hand on the hood. He could sense what an IED was, but anything more sophisticated than that threw him off.

A car full of women in full burqas pulled up, being driven by a man. Brent stood in front of the car as the man said, "No, no."

Brent was going to step away, but he had a feeling. "No," said Brent. "Get them out of the car."

"They are women," said the ANP translator.

"Then get everyone out of the car."

The man protested loudly, while the women muttered and gathered in a group near the car. The ANP opened the trunk, checked the seats. Brent stared unabashedly at the women.

"Don't do that," said the ANP translator, but Brent ignored him.

The three uniformed Army personnel watched Brent, a hand on their weapons.

Brent pointed to a woman in the center of the group. "Ask her what her relationship is to the man."

An ANP corporal asked. The woman answered. Brent started to sweat. He half-expected a man to answer, but not many men would debase themselves to wear a burqa. He felt her as *wrong*.

Brent finally walked up to her. He stared at the veil but couldn't see the woman's eyes. She moved her arm under her burqa.

Brent grabbed it. The woman shrieked. The man ran around the car. Brent pulled her arm behind her while feeling along her side.

He felt part of the explosive vest there.

Brent put up a shield. The man rushed at him but bounced off the shield. Brent did not let go of the woman's arm. He knew he was being lecherous by touching her, but he knew she had a homemade bomb vest underneath.

Brent yelled, "She has a vest bomb."

"She has no bomb," said one of the ANP. One of the soldiers talked to the woman. He put his hand on her back, and his eyes widened. He said something in Pashtun, pulling the woman away.

Then the ANP went into action. The driver also pulled back, away from his vehicle. Brent saw the chaos as they brought the woman into the checkpoint.

Ledbetter came out of the office. "We need their lawyer."

The ANP translated for the driver, "I have no lawyer. What have you done with my daughter!"

"She's under arrest. We're going to —"

The checkpoint's office exploded. Everyone outside ducked, but most of the blast was under a canopy to the left of the small makeshift building.

Brent ran into the smoldering building, thinking she must have decided to wait until she was among more Americans before setting off the bomb. He ran past one of the soldiers who had brought the woman in, being held up by another soldier whose arm was covered in blood.

The office walls had collapsed inward. One man lay on the ground in front of the office, half under a destroyed desk. Brent saw men being carried out from the other room next to the office. On the third side of the office, papers fluttered down onto an upturned desk. Inside the office, he saw a pair of legs half-covered by the burqa. Outside behind the office, an armored Humvee sat parked with no damage to it.

"Fuck," Brent said, turning to the man under the desk.

An Army private covered in blood came up to him. Both men lifted the man on the floor while Brent looked him over quickly.

"You injured?" the private asked Brent.

"No. You?"

"No. We got some of the injured outside."

In the chaos, the driver had taken off, leaving behind the four women who were wailing in either fear or grief. Brent ignored them and went to the first injured man.

They triaged the injured so by the time the ambulance got through, Brent had healed two ANP's that were the most severely injured.

He finished his work on the second ANP and got up. His knees and lower legs were soaked in blood.

"One of ours is dead," said Ledbetter, pointing.

Brent saw four bodies laid out with a shirt or jacket on their faces.

"You put her alone in that office, didn't you?"

"We have no females. Allen was going to call for one to come down." He looked at the bodies. "Shit."

"We got the other women," said the private that helped Brent. "I'll radio up for a female."

Brent said, "They probably don't know anything."

They had stopped wailing and were now being guarded by some very angry ANP.

"We'll take them in anyway," said Ledbetter. "They'll know the man. And we got his registration."

"Or his papers," said Brent. "If you have his papers, I can find him."

"No shit?"

"Magic."

"Hey!" yelled Ledbetter, "Anyone got that fuck's papers?"

As the ANP asked among themselves, Brent hoped and prayed they had something of his. He walked around the checkpoint, when one of the ANP produced a paper. It was a flier the ANP was supposed to pass out for the election.

"He took it and dropped it."

"Better than nothing. I'll try it."

Brent took the paper. He saw the man who gave it to him in his mind's eye. He shoved that image away. He saw the Afghan, angry at getting the paper. He closed his eyes and forced the connection.

"His name is Mehdrad Sahudin. He was going to his brother's house."

"Did he know about the bomb?"

Brent looked up at Ledbetter. "I'm not *that* good."

The ANP walked over to them. "All the women are his daughters. The one who died was the youngest."

"Did they know about the bomb?" asked Ledbetter.

"They say they didn't."

"You don't believe them."

"Women, daughters, are very close. They would know."

Ledbetter said, "Find out where their uncle lives. Send some people there to arrest him."

They heard sirens as the ambulances rolled away. The hearses followed.

Ledbetter said to no one in particular, "If she detonated in the mall, there would have been a shitload of destruction." He nodded to Brent, then went back into the office.

The ANP went off, while Brent stayed at the checkpoint. He wanted to go hunting with the ANP, but none of the other Army men went with them. Someone from the ANP came and picked up the women after dark, an hour before Brent left for the night.

14

CAMP PHOENIX

FOR THE TWO DAYS before the election, Brent manned different checkpoints. On both of those days, the dragons flew over Kabul.

The Afghans didn't know whether to flee or stare. Children looked up constantly for a glimpse of the mighty beasts. When the dragons roared, people ran. In one case, Tyrath set down at a market and took a whole goat, still alive. After the butcher's initial shock, he demanded payment from the government.

Election day, and security stepped up. Brent had to wear his indigo robes. He knew he was going to stick out even more than any UN envoy; it would be obvious who he represented.

"Hamid Karzai has gotten the most death threats," said the archmage. "You will be right near him, as close as you can. You're representing the UN here."

"The UN?"

"It can't be us. We don't want to make it seem like we're throwing the election."

Brent got in a car with a group of UN election officials.

"We'll drop you off at his house," said one with a heavy Norwegian accent.

Karzai's house was a mansion. Guards patted him down.

"What is this?" demanded a voice. A scarred ANA general came out of the house. "Ah, you must be the American sorcerer."

Brent felt fear creep up his chest. He looked like Scar for a split second. But it wasn't him. *Was it?*

He swallowed the fear and held out his hand. "First Magus Brent Rogers."

"Lieutenant General Aminullah Karim. Come inside."

They shook hands went into the cool halls of the mansion. "Sometimes these men, they are too obvious."

Brent thought the translation stone messed up, so he just nodded.

Hamid Karzai was shorter than Brent. Brent shook his hand, found it solid and firm.

"Do you prefer English?" Karzai asked in that language.

"Either Pashtun or English. I have a translation amulet."

"English. I need to keep in practice if I will be working with your country."

"Yes, sir."

"I have many guards," he said, sitting down. He waved Brent to the seat in front of him. "They say you can see the future."

"No, not quite. I can sense when something is wrong. Like a person who's an enemy. Or if there are weapons in the room."

"You found a bomb on a woman at a checkpoint a few days ago."

"Yes, sir. But she was able to set it off."

"Her husband is in jail, along with two other men."

"I thought it was her father —"

He said, "Her father, how do you say, 'turned his coat'?"

"Turncoat. Is a turncoat."

"In exchange for telling us who gave her the vest, we set him free."

"I'd like to know if she was forced to wear it."

"If she was a good wife, she would have done what her husband says."

"Right," said Brent. Women were so subservient here. He wasn't sure if he liked that or not.

"What other magic can you do?"

"Not much else for use in crowded rooms. I can shield you from blasts and bullets. I can set off bombs from a distance."

"Can you shield me in public?"

"I can do that."

"Good. Very good."

So Brent followed him around for the day. He was difficult to guard and shield, as he would constantly go out into a fray of people. Brent was often shoved aside by his regular bodyguards. Finally, Brent just gave up, staying at the end of the line, keeping an eye on him. The man seemed well-guarded anyway.

Instead, Brent paid attention to his surroundings. The crowds hid guns, but, if he concentrated, he knew he could sense any enemies that might be packing. However, to concentrate on that, he needed to be still. Unfortunately, he was jostled constantly. Karzai stopped in different places to show his ink-stained finger proving that he voted and giving it to the Taliban as he spoke.

Nothing happened, thankfully, except once, when he saw Tyrath in the sky, screaming his fury and making people look up or flee in terror.

At the end of it all, the UN dropped him off at Camp Phoenix, as the convoy dwindled down to two cars. He didn't even get a thank you.

Brent paused and took a deep breath before heading into the compound. He could hear gunfire and fireworks outside, but he just wanted to sit.

Makrah came running up to him from out of nowhere. "Listen! Listen to that!"

"What?" said Brent, yawning.

Makrah grinned as Tyrath came up, his usual somber self. "Listen to them celebrating!"

"Yeah. It's their first real election."

"I will go out to celebrate freedom! Come with us."

"Are you crazy?"

"I knew he would say something like that," said Tyrath. "It is dangerous."

Makrah grabbed Brent by the arm. "We will not stay out long."

Tyrath shook his head. Brent sighed. "Fine, we'll go."

Makrah led the way out of the compound. He acted like an excited little kid.

Just outside, a knot of people gathered, waving Afghan flags and yelling things in Pashtun. Brent watched as Makrah went right up to them. They welcomed him like some long-lost brother, patting him on the back and talking to him.

Brent stayed a little bit away, watching Makrah.

"This seems to be what he wants," said Tyrath.

The group then broke out into song — probably their national anthem, Brent guessed — with Makrah joining in. Brent couldn't help but smile.

Then the group enveloped Brent and Tyrath, shaking their hands and patting them on the back and shoulders.

Makrah said in Brent's ear, "They thank you for what you do."

Brent shrugged. "I didn't do much."

"They saw you on the television."

Great, thought Brent. He forced a smile and shook hands.

Eventually some guards came out and the group dispersed quietly. Brent really needed food and a place to sit. He went back into the compound with a somber Tyrath and an elated Makrah.

"They are so happy," Makrah said.

"So you'll stay?"

"I will stay to help, not to hurt."

Brent patted Makrah's shoulder. "Tell that to Archmage Deiter. I'm sure we can find some humanitarian places for you." He looked at Tyrath. "What about you?"

"I will fight in Iraq. Too many rules here."

"That's the Army for you. Too many rules."

Tyrath said to Makrah, "This was your idea."

"Yes, and wonderful, is it not?"

Tyrath snorted.

Brent swayed. "Look, I've been guarding Karzai all day. I need some rest."

"We will leave you." Makrah clapped Brent's forearm in an ancient gesture of friendship. "Until we meet again."

"You're leaving now?"

"It is after the election. You will be under new orders."

Brent chuckled. "Things don't happen that fast in the Army."

Brent bid the two dragons farewell and headed to the barracks. He was too tired to take a shower, though now would be the perfect time of night to do it. If he was lucky, he would be able to sleep in his clothes for a couple of hours before reveille, after which he would see Makrah off and find out his new orders.

He tumbled into his cot, fully clothed, just as the door to the barracks burst open and Tyrath yelled, "Wizard!"

"Shh!" Brent called and struggled up.

The generator lights were on, casting the barracks in a dim yellow glow. Tyrath threaded his way through toward the cot. Brent met him in the middle of the barracks. He dragged Tyrath outside to not disturb the sleeping soldiers men.

"Where is my box?" Tyrath demanded.

"What box?"

"My collection."

"Didn't you bring it with you to the tent with the Archmage?"

"Yes, but it's gone from there." Tyrath was beyond agitated; his body was tense and the look on his face full of worry and fear.

"I don't have it," said Brent when they got outside. "I'll help you look for it."

"Makrah is trying to find the Archmage."

"Did you look all around the tent you were in? Maybe someone moved it?"

"I didn't sense it in the tent."

"You can sense it if you're close?"

"Yes."

"Let's go walk around, then."

Brent walked with Tyrath deeper into the compound, away from the barracks and into the area of the compound itself, the section that was open 24/7 in support of the ANP in Kabul. Task Force Tiger Claw hung out in the HQ, smoking while waiting for anything to happen tonight.

"I sense nothing here," Tyrath said, as they walked past the men.

They headed to the depot, where the vehicles were locked up behind a fence with barbed wire.

Tyrath paused. "Something." He tried the gate but it was locked with a padlock and chain. He shook it.

Brent noted soldiers watching them. "Tyrath, you can't go in there."

Tyrath suddenly dropped to his knees with a grunt. He held onto the chain link fence, as Brent reached out to touch Tyrath's back. He was covered in scales. Tyrath growled and shook Brent's hand off, letting go of the chain and rolling onto the ground.

"Get away!" he yelled.

Tyrath started to glow, a bright orange light all around him. Brent could feel the heat radiate from him. He stepped back a few paces and turned his head away.

When Brent looked back, he could see the black smoke and Tyrath rising, lifting his head to glare at Brent. He tilted his head back. Brent started, then realized he was going to belch fire.

Brent automatically summoned the shield, throwing his hands forward as if to push. A wall of ice suddenly appeared before him. At the same time, a blast of fire burst at the wall of ice, melting some of it into a pool of mud. Brent kept his head bent and his hands up. He felt the cold air of the wall against his shield.

The roar of the fire stopped. Tyrath tried to climb over the ice wall instead, but Makrah, in dragon form, tackled Tyrath, knocking him into and through the depot fence.

Brent turned and ran toward HQ while Army and Marines poured out of the building.

"Jesus Christ —" "What the fuck!"

"Get the Archmage!" Brent turned back at the fighting dragons in the depot behind him.

Makrah wrapped his blue snake-like body around Tyrath's red lizard one. But Tyrath struggled, trying to get one arm free. He seemed to be glowing red.

Tyrath moved his head, roared flame at Makrah's face. Makrah didn't burn or melt. He turned his head to the side, getting the brunt of the flame against the side of his face. He seemed to tighten his hold on Tyrath.

Tyrath bit down on Makrah's neck, just below his jaw. Bright blue luminescent liquid burst from between his jaws, jetting into the air. Makrah opened his mouth and more of the liquid flowed, pooling onto the ground.

Tearing away flesh and gore, Tyrath got an arm free. He bit down again, this time at Makrah's face, tearing out an eye.

Tyrath shrugged out of Makrah's embrace. He looked toward the chapel, took two steps toward it. He stopped and roared, as if in agony, and whipped his head around toward HQ.

"Run!" someone yelled, and the grunts bolted.

Some ran inside, some ran left and right. Brent ran left while three soldiers dove behind crates the moment Tyrath let loose with fire. Brent got the shield up to protect himself and the two guys nearest him. The third Army guy who ran past the reach of the shield caught fire, and, when the burst of flame stopped, there was nothing left, not even ashes.

Brent realized Tyrath didn't go after HQ or the other soldiers.

"He's after me," Brent yelled at them. "You guys get out of here!"

The two soldiers jumped up and ran toward barracks. Brent watched as Tyrath kept trying to go to the chapel, but seemed to be pushed away, back toward Brent. Something was in that chapel that Tyrath wanted.

Tyrath lumbered toward Brent. He wished he still had his staff.

He had to run in front of Tyrath to the chapel across the aisle. There was only one way he could get there. Brent closed his eyes, clenched his hands into fists, and concentrated on slipping into the spirit world.

He knew he was in the spirit world when he opened his eyes and Tyrath wasn't in front of him. He only wanted to "teleport" — move quickly from one side to the other. He saw the bright light of the chapel reflected in the spirit world, so he ran for it, running around the ghosts that still inhabited Camp Phoenix. He knew when he reappeared, he'd be disoriented at least, exhausted at worst.

Brent concentrated again and reappeared before the chapel. He had just missed the steps — he could have ended up with his foot embedded in the wooden step. He reached for the door and threw it open, diving into the building.

"Well, well, if it isn't the War Mage."

Brent raised his dizzy head. Lieutenant Waters — Starforce — stood in the aisle of the chapel. He held a large gold cross with a short line through the top of the cross. The cross glowed red.

Behind Lieutenant Waters sat Tyrath's box, open and spilling out the same kinds of gold crosses along the floor. Brent got to his hands and knees as Waters approached.

"You think you're the most powerful wizard? When I eat your heart, you won't be."

The doors burst open and Tyrath's head filled the frame. He roared, filling the room with a sound almost as loud as an explosion. Brent covered his ears as Tyrath tried to shoulder his way into the wooden building.

Waters backed up, but Tyrath couldn't get his bulk into the building.

"Kill him!" Waters yelled, raising the gold cross over his head.

At the new orders, Tyrath turned to Brent.

Brent's dizziness had changed to a full-blown headache. He could only think of parts of spells, nothing coherent. As Tyrath inhaled, Brent raised his hands again. The fire came at him, and he gave it a mental push.

The fire turned away from him, flowing across the pews toward Waters. The fire wasn't as hot as if it came directly from Tyrath, but it was still an accelerant on everything it touched. That included Waters.

Tyrath's fire poured onto Waters, engulfing him and his cross. Tyrath didn't stop, Brent kept pushing, his eyes blinded with the exertion. He ignored Waters' screaming, as he wandered into the burning pews, falling, burning.

The fire stopped finally. Brent brought his hands down, while the chapel burned. He ran out the door while Tyrath changed into a human. Naked, he ran into the burning building.

"Tyrath! No!" Brent reached for him, but Tyrath ran past him.

The front part of the building collapsed. Someone grabbed Brent to pull him back.

Then, a man came out of the fire, carrying an armful of gold Eastern Orthodox crosses, glinting in the firelight. Tyrath walked forward, as if walking on burning wood was a walk on dew kissed grass.

He dropped the crosses at Brent's feet. "I am your servant," he said.

"No, Tyrath. I am your friend."

Tyrath looked Brent in the eye. "Friend." He smiled for once.

It didn't look any better in the morning. Archmage Deiter gazed at the ice wall that had been Makrah's body stretched out along the depot. The fence lay destroyed, along with eight out of the two dozen vehicles in the immediate vicinity of the fence.

"Where is Tyrath?" Deiter asked as Brent stood next to him.

"He wants to go to Iraq."

Deiter frowned and put his hands behind his back. "I don't think that's such a good idea."

"Sir, if I might ask, are the dragons in Iraq under our control?"

"Yes."

Which explained how Waters knew how to control Tyrath. Brent looked at the ice and the dragons' talk of freedom. "Tyrath wouldn't want that."

"I know. That's why I don't think it's a good idea." He turned to Brent. "I'll tell Captain Laurence that there's no more Fifth Wing here to command. You tell Tyrath to leave, abandon the war, just get the hell out of here."

"Yes, sir," said Brent.

Brent walked back to barracks. It was empty, the men having gone to patrol Kabul. Tyrath was the only person inside, sitting on Brent's cot. He was handling one of those foot-long gold crosses, caressing it. He looked up at Brent's entrance.

"Fifth Wing's been disbanded. You're free to go."

Tyrath looked away for a moment. "I will return to Russia."

"Maybe I could get you to stay here if you want."

"No. I will go home." He stood up. He glanced down at the cross. Then he thrust it out at Brent. "When you need me, call me with this."

Brent took it. "I hope I never have to use it."

Tyrath inclined his head. He turned and walked out the door, not looking back.

Brent passed the cross through his hands, examining the etched lines along the sides. He turned to the postal box with the Matchbox cars, the bone from Olron's death, and put the cross on top. He found a piece of paper and a pen, scribbled a note, and placed that on top.

Chrissie —

Hold onto these until I get back home.

Love,
Brent

ABOUT THE AUTHOR

L. A. Jacob has been writing since she could hold a pencil and draw a straight line. She wrote fan fiction before branching out into novels and short stories. After her first book was published, she wrote five more within the span of three years. She is also the author of *Real Magic for Writers*.

Interested in magic(k), cards, and divination, she lives in Rhode Island with her son and three cats. You can find out more about L. A. Jacob at her website, *lajacob.com*.

ALSO BY THE AUTHOR

GRIMAULKIN

BOOK ONE IN THE "GRIMAULKIN" SERIES

by L. A. Jacob

Treading the straight and narrow is not natural to one who summons demons.

HOMECOMING

A "WAR MAGE" NOVEL

by Jake Logan

Even wizards in the U.S. armed forces have to go home some time.

Available from Water Dragon Publishing in
hardcover, trade paperback, digital, and audio editions
waterdragonpublishing.com

CARNIVAL FARM

by Lisa Jacob

When a local veterinarian decides to take over a traveling carnival's petting zoo, she doesn't realize the insanity behind the scenes.

Available from Paper Angel Press in
hardcover, trade paperback, digital, and audio editions
paperangelpress.com